GREYMIST FAIR

FRANCESCA ZAPPIA

GREYMIST FAIR

Greenwillow Books,
An Imprint of HarperCollins*Publishers*

Greymist Fair
Text copyright © 2023 by Francesca Zappia
Title page, part opener, and page 316 illustrations copyright © 2023 by Julia Iredale
Jacket hand lettering copyright © 2023 by Holly Dunn
All other illustrations copyright © 2023 by Francesca Zappia

The text of this book is set in Chaparral Pro Light.
Book design by Sylvie Le Floc'h

Library of Congress Cataloging-in-Publication Data is available.
ISBN 978-0-06-316169-6 (hardcover)

23 24 25 26 27 LBC 5 4 3 2 1
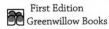
First Edition
Greenwillow Books

ANNABELLE DIRR

*For Annabelle and Adalynn
and future generations*

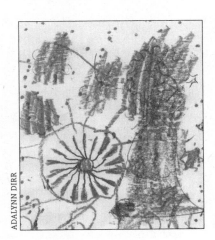

ADALYNN DIRR

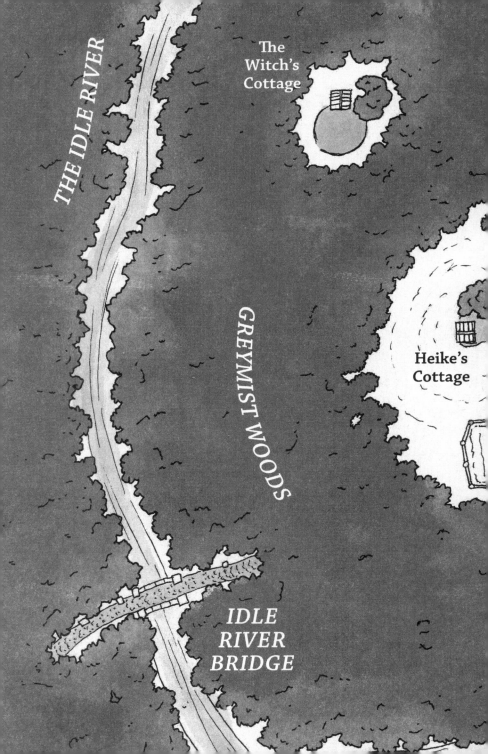

Greymist Fair

Northern
Fields

Greymist
Manor

The
Inn

Fisherman's
Hut

The Inlet

GREY LAKE

"I don't have the heart to leave my children in the forest. The wild beasts would soon come and tear them apart."

"And when the full moon had risen, Hansel took his little sister by the hand and followed the pebbles which shone like newly minted silver pieces and showed them the way."

"Hansel and Gretel,"
The Complete Fairy Tales of the Brothers Grimm

CAST OF CHARACTERS

The Children

Heike (tailor)

Wenzel (innkeeper)

Liesel

Katrina

Fritz

Hans

Villagers

Hilda (tailor)

Doctor Death (doctor)

Ulrich (carpenter) – Gabi (midwife)

Tomas (carpenter's apprentice)

Gottfried (hunter) – Oswald

The Duke (dog)

Johanna (baker) – Dagny (baker)

Lord Greymist – Lady Greymist

Falk (fisherman)

Jürgen (butcher)

Elma Klein (farmer) – Norbert Klein

Ada Bosch

Oliver

Curt

Godric (blacksmith)

Albert Schafer (shepherd)

Travelers

Prince Altan

Evren (prince's aide)

Jocasta (caravan leader)

Omar (caravan guide)

Others

Death

TABLE OF
CONTENTS

HOME

A road leads into a dark forest. It passes through a village some travelers never see. The village is not meant for everyone. To outsiders, it's a place of darkness and whispers, threatened by bright-eyed creatures that live in the wood. Its people are friendly, but insular; its routines familiar, but not inclusive.

A tall man in a dark coat walks the road. Death follows on his heels. Greymist Fair is their home, but only one of them is welcome. The man is a doctor, a healer. Death can only ever be themself. Curious eyes and spiteful hearts follow them through the forest but do not touch them; the road is safe. The doctor and Death don't waste any time; there are many who need the doctor's help.

The village's noble family.

The widowed fisherman and his son.

The orphans in the wind-slanted shack.

The butcher, inspecting his many knives.

The kind old innkeepers and the abandoned boy.

And the tailor. Always, the tailor. She is not ailing or hurt, and the doctor will make sure she stays that way.

As they walk, Death hums a tune. It's a popular rhyme with the children of Greymist Fair. When they approach the outskirts of the village, Death stops while the doctor continues on. Gradually the village emerges from the mist. Cozy fires burn on cobbled hearths, walls and roofs thatched tight against the darkness. Neighbors trade wares and stories. They keep one another company in the long lulls between visitors, and on the nights when they are sure evil is real, and it lives in the forest.

The doctor wishes he could calm their fears, but he would have to lie to them. He, better than anyone else, knows that Death waits in the trees. That Death is patient. And that Death will do anything to return home.

THE GIRL
WHO OUTRAN
DEATH

one

Only one road led to Greymist Fair. It cut a winding path through the forest, wide enough for two horse-drawn carts to pass side by side, or for six men to walk comfortably without their shoulders touching. Large stones paved it all the way from one misty edge of the forest to the other, and on one side of the road iron lanterns hung on iron hooks, illuminating the path with a spectral blue light that never went out.

When Heike was very young, her mother had led her out of the village and down the west road. The heels of her mother's boots made a solid thumping on the stones in time with the rustling of her bright skirts. Heike, her small hand sweating in her mother's grasp, hurried to keep up. Mist crept from between the tree trunks on either side of the road but never moved past the glow of the lanterns.

As the last cottages of Greymist Fair disappeared behind them, Heike's mother stopped and kneeled beside her.

"Listen to me, Henrike." Hilda was calm and spoke softly.

"It's okay to come down the road. As long as you don't stray from the path, you will always be able to find your way home, and nothing bad will happen to you." She released Heike's hands and began to retie the small red ribbon at the end of Heike's braid. Her mother had quick, deft fingers, tailor's fingers, and the ribbon went back in place without a strand of hair slipping free. "If you leave the road, there are creatures in the woods that would steal you away and eat you up," her mother said, tugging the end of Heike's braid just once, gentle but firm. "You must never go into the woods, Heike. Do you understand?"

"But you go into the woods," Heike said, suddenly uncomfortable with her back to the trees.

"I do," said her mother. "I go to speak to the witch, to make sure she and her wargs stay far away from you and everyone else in the village. I can run very fast, and that keeps me safe."

Her mother had let Heike turn and peer between the tree trunks to see that there was nothing there, and then led her back to Greymist Fair.

When her mother was still alive, Heike had no reason to leave the village. After her mother's death, she went only as far down the road as necessary. It had been two years. Heike was eighteen now, and she still wondered, sometimes, if she would ever see a glimpse of her mother between the trees. Either the ghost of who she had been, or the shadow of the warg she'd become.

The afternoon was cool. Heike marched along the west road at a brisk pace, her berry basket swinging in one hand and her satchel slung across her chest and slapping against her thigh. It was early enough in the day that the light of the lanterns was unnecessary, but still they stood lit along the road, keeping the mist off the stones. Though sunlight never breached the canopy of the trees, the forest had its own kind of light, a muted brightness. Cries of mysterious animals echoed from deep in the wood. Heike focused on the swishing of her skirts and the *thump-thump-thump* of her boots. She'd inherited most of her clothes from her mother, including the bright skirts and the boots that never seemed to wear thin, and having them made her feel safe.

She'd heard some travelers say that the road to Greymist Fair took only hours to traverse, while others said days. Some said they'd met merchants and adventurers who had walked the entire length of the road and never found the village, despite that the road ran straight through it. For Heike, the trip out of the village to the bridge over the Idle River took an hour and a half if she walked quickly, and the trip back the same time.

Not ten paces to the left of the bridge, partially cloaked in the dense underbrush of the forest, was a large redberry bush. A week ago she'd found the bushes along the road bearing fruit, though it was nearing winter now and they only bore fruit in spring. There had been a bush on the right side of the bridge as well, even closer to the road, that she'd tried to dig up and replant near her cottage. But the bush had grown small and sickly, never producing any fruit, as if taking it from the forest had drained the life from it.

Today the Idle River flowed lazily under the stone bridge, like it could feel winter approaching and was preparing to hibernate. Heike stepped off the road and hurried to the redberry bush, flicking her basket open and plucking berries the size of her thumb with trembling fingers. Her legs shook, her stomach twitched, and she pressed her lips together to hold in her nervous giggles. A bird fluttered off a branch overhead. Heike snapped the basket shut and jumped back on the road, where she started to laugh, bracing her hands on her knees to keep herself from collapsing.

When she righted herself again, she peeked inside the basket. It was only half full. It would barely be enough to make the rich red dye her mother had loved so much; she needed more if she wanted a darker color. The skin on the back of Heike's neck prickled. She looked down the road in the direction of Greymist Fair, where the lanterns cast the forest in blue and silver. Then she looked the other way, over the crest of the Idle River Bridge.

The creeping sensation worked its way over her shoulders and down her arms. There were more bushes on the other side of the bridge, full of berries that hadn't spoiled even after a week, and some were close to the road. It wouldn't hurt to check.

Heike started over the bridge. The Idle River lolled cold and deep beneath it, its banks overhung with moss and tree roots. Here, the canopy of trees overhead disappeared to expose a strip of gray sky. Even the harsh depths of winter wouldn't freeze the Idle, and Heike had heard more than one story from Falk the fisherman about the bodies of unlucky travelers who had fallen into the Idle and turned up in Grey Lake. They usually caught on the roots on the banks or washed up on shore, bloated and pale, eyes chewed out by the fishes, and they smelled as rotten as they looked.

The smell of rotten flesh reached Heike now as she crested the bridge. Her imagination was good, but not that good, not even when her nerves were already standing on end. The road stretched out past the bridge, lined with lanterns, and the trees arched overhead again until their branches twisted together. A dark shape sprawled beneath the lantern closest to the bridge. Heike descended carefully, hugging the opposite side of the road as she crept closer.

The shape was clothing, arranged in the shape of a man, as

if he'd leaped from the bridge and landed badly. Thick dark wool pants and the scraps of a torn linen shirt, and blood and viscera leaking into the cracks between the stones. Empty boots. There was no body.

Heike pressed her hand to her mouth as she gagged. She knew those shoes; she'd finished making them just last week. They belonged to Tomas, apprentice to the carpenter, and he was two years younger than her. Several days before, he had installed a new sign for Heike's tailoring business outside her cottage. He'd carved it himself.

There was only one thing in the woods that killed and left clothing behind: the witch's evil creatures, the wargs.

Heike wiped her mouth and searched the trees nearby. The stillness of the forest betrayed no stalkers, but her mother had not raised a fool. So when Heike turned back for Greymist Fair, she ran.

two

The houses and cottages of Greymist Fair clustered in a shallow valley, stitched together by cobblestone streets and warm lamps on crooked posts. Firelight spilled from dusty windows. Wildflowers grew in planters outside doors, lovingly tended and allowed to twirl and twist up along the faces of the cottages.

Heike sprinted up the west road, past the sign welcoming travelers to Greymist Fair, past the first homes. Behind one, a large, happy cow chewed cud. Atop the next perched a row of blackbirds that watched Heike pass with disgruntled croaks. She entered the town proper, flying past Ada Bosch and the seven children she led, hand in hand; past Gottfried, carrying his polished hunting rifle and followed by his loping Great Dane, The Duke; then into the village square, where Heike's friend, Wenzel, stood sweeping the stone steps of the inn and singing songs they'd learned together as children, when things were simpler and Wenzel was known by a different name.

When he saw her go by, he yelled, "Heike? Heike!"

She continued past the great stone well that stood in the center of Greymist Fair and out to the opposite side of the village, where the cottages dotted the northern hills. The home of Ulrich the carpenter was largest, and the farthest north, up against a small swath of cleared forest. Ulrich himself stood outside at the top of his hill, splitting logs. A burly man with dark skin, a thick beard, and a healthy respect for the forest, Ulrich was one of the few people in Greymist Fair who ventured into the woods. He lowered his axe when he saw her climbing toward him.

"It's Tomas!" she gasped as soon as she knew he'd hear. Her hair hung in sweaty tangles around her face, and the ribbon had nearly slipped off the end of her braid. "Tomas is . . . on the west road . . . he's . . ." She put her hands on her knees as her torso cramped. The image of the blood floated before her. She was used to seeing blood and smelling rotten meat, but not from a human. She couldn't stop herself from vomiting straight onto the scuffed toes of Ulrich's boots. Ulrich dropped his axe and put a large, warm hand on her shoulder.

"Henrike. Speak slower. What happened to Tomas?"

She told him what she'd found. As soon as she'd finished, he was off, dropping his axe and rushing behind his cottage. Heike slumped next to his pile of wood. Numbness filled her from her hips to her feet. She pulled the ribbon from her hair with cold fingers and combed through her braid. Ulrich came back moments later on his horse, with his wood cart hitched behind, and started down the hill and into the village.

From where she sat, Heike could now see people emerging into the streets, talking, pointing the way she'd gone and up toward Ulrich's. Ulrich disappeared between the buildings. A moment later he reappeared as a dark speck on the west road before he disappeared again between the trees, followed by several other men.

"Heike!"

Wenzel's long legs brought him swiftly up the hillside. His brown skin had turned wan with worry, his dark eyebrows pushed together over his warm brown eyes.

"Don't come too near," Heike called. "I might vomit on you as well."

"What happened? Ulrich said something about a murder when he passed by, told me to call Doctor Death." Wenzel took in her sweaty face, her muddy boots, her tousled hair. "On second thought, let's get to the inn, and then you can tell me."

"I don't know if I can walk," she said.

Wenzel turned, kneeled, and motioned to his back. "Hop on."

They had done this when they were younger, but as children it had been Heike carrying the smaller Wenzel on her back. Taking his shoulders, she pulled herself up. She relaxed to the bounce of his stride and his arms holding her legs. Her berry basket jolted against his stomach. Johanna and Dagny, the baker wives, gave them strange looks as they passed, first at Heike's bunched-up skirts and then at Heike herself. The apothecary startled and dropped his armful of herbs when he saw them.

Heike hid her face in Wenzel's shoulder. She hadn't expected anything less. Her mother had gone so often into the forest to appease the witch, the villagers had kept their distance from her. Heike had never gone into the woods and had never seen the witch, but her mother's reputation had passed right down to her, just like her clothes, her profession, and the color of her eyes. To the villagers, the witch was a servant of death, and anyone who associated with her was just as bad.

They reached the front steps of the inn. Heike said, "Put me down."

Wenzel shouldered his way through the front door. "Not yet."

"I can walk."

"I know you can."

Without any travelers, the inn sat empty and unused, Wenzel its only occupant. A draft cut through the darkened great room. Wenzel carried Heike past the log desk, past the staircase that led to the second floor, past the empty chairs and tables. Papers full of scrawled handwriting were scattered across one table, Wenzel's jotted notes of stories he'd collected over the years. He set her down in an armchair by the hearth, and she dropped her berry basket. In a minute Wenzel had a small fire crackling at her feet. He hurried off again, behind the staircase to the kitchen, and returned a moment later with a mug of warm milk. Several times Heike began to tell him to sit still, but the words never escaped her. She was not prepared to deny Wenzel his nurturing tendencies.

"Don't call Doctor Death," she said. "I'll be fine soon."

Wenzel shook his head and pulled up a second armchair. "Now, what happened?"

She explained as she sipped, considerably calmer. As Wenzel listened, his face turned greener and greener, and he covered his mouth with his hand. Heike kept the details to a minimum, but Wenzel had always been squeamish at the mention of violence.

The more Heike talked, the less real the scene on the road felt. She must have looked at the boots only for a second or two, long enough to confirm they belonged to Tomas. The memory felt like a berry dying on the vine; even now its innards were rotting away, leaving only a husk. It felt like someone else's memory from another time.

"But . . . Tomas." Wenzel sat back. "The wargs. It had to be."

"But on the road? The road is supposed to be safe."

"Then you think a person did it? Why leave the clothes?"

"Maybe they wanted to make it look like a warg killed him."

Wenzel turned toward the fire. His frown deepened. "Warg or not, what if it's still out there? What if it had hurt you, too?"

"It didn't, and wondering about *what if*s isn't going to solve what happened. People go down that road all the time and they don't get torn open. It's not normal."

"But the things in the forest—"

"There have always been dangerous things in the forest. The road is supposed to be safe."

She caught Wenzel's gaze over the rim of her mug. "What about Katrina?" he said. "And what about your mother?"

Heike went very still. The fire flickered low. "They weren't on the road."

"But they did die the way you said. Didn't they?" Wenzel cleared his throat, fingers flexing against the arm of his chair.

"Ulrich was the one who found Katrina and my mother," Heike said. "And all he found of them was tattered clothing and their shoes. No blood, he said. Maybe he'll know if the same thing did this to Tomas." She stood and held her mug out for Wenzel. The strength had returned to her legs, and she had a sudden desire to be by herself to think. "I need to prepare this dye. I'll be back once Ulrich returns—I'm sure he'll have questions for me."

"Wait." Wenzel caught her arm. "Let me go with you. It's so close to the forest."

"I live plenty far from the trees. And nothing has ever come into the village before—why would it now?"

"Why would it attack anything on the road, either?"

Heike didn't respond. Looking unhappy, Wenzel took the mug from her and let her go.

Heike's cottage had once belonged to her mother, and to her mother's mother before her. It sat on a hill just behind the inn, up a dirt path and beneath the wide branches of an old and twisted linden tree. Tied to the door was a bundle of sage, holly, and chamomile, something her mother had put up that Heike now kept out of habit. At the door, Heike could see the shepherd's flock grazing beneath the gray sky, and past them, Ulrich's home on its own hill in the north. To her right, in the south, was Elma Klein's farm, where the winter wheat was poking from the ground in green shoots.

To the west was the edge of the forest. Wind ruffled the treetops. The trees seemed to loom up as if climbing the hillside. She shivered, wishing she'd taken Wenzel up on his offer, and ducked inside.

The cottage was one small room divided into two sections. In the smaller was the heavy iron washtub, the oak dresser carved by her great-great-grandmother, and the bed in which Heike had slept with her mother when she was a child.

The larger section held all her mother's tailoring tools, some now largely unused. A tall, upright loom, the biggest instrument she owned, stood against the back wall. Heike had spent more time learning how to repair it than she had using it. Beside it on the floor was a pot where she kept her distaffs, and a smaller pot on the table nearby that had become a repository of spindles. She had baskets and baskets of wool and linen, a bit already dyed and a bit kept aside for times like these when she found rare colors. She had boxes of needles made of wood, iron, and bone, some of them warped so badly she couldn't use them; boxes of pins of different shapes and sizes, some plain and easy to lose in the fabric, others fixed with bright but chipped jewels on their ends; boxes of thimbles, some so old the dimples had near worn away. There was a fireplace where she boiled water to make dyes, and beside that, the worktable where her mother had kept her tools for shoemaking.

Heike's mother had taught her how to make shoes by having her make them for Wenzel. He'd been raised by the previous keepers of the inn, a kind elderly couple who had no children's clothing. Heike's mother had provided them with everything they'd needed in exchange for food and someone to watch Heike when she went into the woods, and she'd used the making of Wenzel's clothes to teach Heike what she knew.

Her mother had done the best work in the village, but there were others who knew how to spin, weave, sew, and cobble, and so most villagers avoided the witch-speaker who lived so near to the trees. Her mother had kept food in Heike's stomach by doing work for the innkeepers and by selling goods to the traveling merchants and adventurers who came to Greymist Fair. Her remains—the tattered clothing, her old boots—had been found in the forest, close to those of Katrina, a girl who had been Heike's age. They were killed by the wargs of Greymist, everyone said; spirits of the forest, loyal to the witch, that preyed on any who entered their domain. The wargs would make sense, because anyone who died of violence in Greymist Fair became a warg themselves, leaving no corpse behind.

Heike sat at the worktable by the empty fireplace and did her best to gather herself. Her mother had died four years ago, but it felt like today. It felt like it had been her mother's clothing she'd found on the road. She'd never seen the scene herself—Ulrich wouldn't let her. She'd only seen the small gravestone with her mother's name carved on it, marking a grave with no body.

Preparing the berries and her dye pot took away some of her nerves, at least for a short time. She'd already cleaned the wool she planned to use, and it had been tucked carefully away in a linen bag she kept below the worktable. While the berries boiled over the fire, she took the prepared wool from the bag and ran her fingers over it, then held it close and smelled it. Her mother had smelled like wool and berry dyes and bone needles. She'd never cursed her lack of work, or how far they felt from the village. Heike rested her head on the edge of the worktable and looked down at the muddied toes of her boots. Her mother could make boots that lasted twenty years, but she couldn't make the village accept her.

Boiling the berries seemed to take a lifetime, and as she finished straining the dark crimson water, shouts from the village came in through the open window. She dumped her wool into the pot with the dye, left it over the fire, and took off running back toward the inn.

three

Ulrich had returned. Sitting up on his horse, he looked like a man carved from stone, his eyes shadowed and his thick beard masking the stern set of his jaw. His cart was empty. Gottfried, with his gun and his Great Dane, and Jürgen, the butcher, had followed Ulrich into the forest and now trailed behind the cart. Gottfried looked paler than usual, and Jürgen's ruddy face was unreadable. Ulrich rode through the center of the village and past it, toward his cottage.

Heike stood with Wenzel outside the inn. As Ulrich passed, he'd looked down at them and said, "Find Liesel, please. Bring her to me."

Liesel was Tomas's older sister. They'd lived together in the home that had belonged to their parents, like everyone in Greymist Fair, but while Tomas had never shied away from playing where Heike was, Liesel had heeded her parents' wishes and stayed away. Liesel was already outside in the road, watching the villagers congregate, when Heike and Wenzel found her. Her gaze snapped to Heike.

"It's Tomas, isn't it?" she said. Her voice was stronger than Heike had expected, though her eyes were red. "He didn't come home yesterday."

"Ulrich asked for you."

Liesel followed them north to Ulrich's. Ulrich and Gottfried were outside the barn, staring into the back of the cart. Ulrich's wife, Gabi, stood nearby with one hand on her forehead and one on her hip, looking flustered. Jürgen waited by the barn doors, arms crossed over his expansive stomach, with his son, Hans, who was Heike and Wenzel's age. Hans mimicked his father's posture, though where Jürgen could have taken up the entirety of the barn door, Hans could have slipped through them while they were closed. None of his clothes had ever quite fit his thin and reedy frame. His gaze fixed first on Wenzel and then on Heike as they came up the hill.

"Liesel," Gabi said as they drew near, "I'm so sorry, dear."

Liesel went straight to the cart. "Can I see him?"

"Not much to see," Ulrich said. He motioned to the cart, which held the ragged remains of a linen shirt, pants, and shoes. "When was the last time you saw Tomas? What was he doing?"

Liesel's expression was unreadable. "Yesterday morning. He left before sunrise to come here."

"He never arrived," Ulrich said. "Gottfried, you're usually out in the mornings. Did you see him?"

Gottfried, who had huddled into his coat like a turtle, his neat black hair bristling around his collar, said, "No. Normally I do see him come along the road on my way to the bakery, but Oswald and I were . . ."—he cleared his throat—"busy yesterday morning."

Ulrich grunted.

"Why do you need to ask questions, Ulrich?" Jürgen shifted his huge body away from the barn. Hans glided along in his shadow, his blue eyes flicking to Heike. "You said yourself this is exactly what happened to Hilda and Katrina."

Liesel made a small noise and put a hand over her mouth.

"*Jürgen.*" Gabi motioned toward Heike.

Jürgen scoffed. "She knows good and well what happened to her mother, and so do we. We all know who did this. That damned witch. We've left her alone in the forest all this time and now she's come for us."

They all looked at Heike then as if she might transform into the witch herself. Wenzel took her hand in his.

"You're sure of how you found him?" Ulrich asked. "There was no body at all? Just the blood?"

"The blood and the smell. I didn't think anything was left of the body at all after the wargs' attack."

"Nothing is. This was something else."

Heike realized there was another meaning to Ulrich's questions. Coldly she said, "I didn't do this."

"No, I didn't mean that, of course, Heike." Ulrich's voice went soft. "Did you see anything else nearby? Anything moving in the trees? Did you hear any strange sounds?"

"Why were you that far down the road, anyway?" asked Hans, sounding more curious than accusatory.

"I didn't hear or see anything," Heike said. "I was there for the berries. There are ripe redberries in the forest, far out of season. I went to look for bushes close to the road so that I could gather some for dye."

"Dye for what?" Hans asked.

"Does it matter?" Heike snapped. She squeezed Wenzel's hand, holding back the urge to punch Hans, something she'd wanted to do often when they were children. Her anger had never been able to penetrate Hans's blank expressions, his absolute lack of concern for anyone but himself. Wenzel rubbed her knuckles to bring some heat to her cold fingers.

"We'll call the village to a meeting," Ulrich said. "We need to decide what action to take, if any."

"Where?" asked Gottfried. "Since Lord and Lady Greymist passed, the manor has been closed off."

Wenzel stepped forward. "At the inn. There's plenty of room."

Ulrich nodded. "Let's spread the word, then." He glanced at Jürgen. "We are not sowing rumors or opinions. We'll let the village decide how this should be handled."

Gabi collected Liesel and turned her toward the cottage. Heike pulled Wenzel away from the others, back toward the village center, very aware of Hans's gaze on her as they departed. On their way down the road, they called out to anyone they passed about the meeting, then continued south through the village until they reached the Klein farm. Someone ran down to the lake to tell the fisherman and his son. Clusters of villagers began moving toward the inn, and Heike and Wenzel hurried back to build up the fire in the great room and clear out a space where Ulrich could stand to speak.

Ulrich arrived with Gabi, Liesel, Jürgen, and Hans. Gottfried and Oswald arrived behind Johanna and Dagny, the baker wives. Falk the fisherman, his son, Fritz, and Elma and Norbert Klein came in with many of the workers from Elma's farm. Wenzel pulled over a table for Ulrich to climb on so everyone could see him. When Heike was sure the entire village was there, a tall, dark figure appeared in the doorway, and the crowd in the back parted to allow him to enter.

Doctor Death, dressed all in black, took a place against the back wall. He would have blended with the shadows if not for his pale skin and golden hair. Heike didn't know where he had been or who had told him about the meeting, but she wasn't surprised to see him. He always seemed to know when something wasn't right.

Ulrich shifted, making the table creak beneath him, and cleared his throat. Heike, hidden behind Ulrich, in the corner by the fireplace, was just glad no one was looking at her.

Ulrich cleared his throat again and quieted the room.

"Evidence of the death of my young apprentice, Tomas, was found on the west road today," he said.

The faces in the crowd were pale, nervous. There came a few light gasps at Tomas's name, but none at the mention of death. Death was well known in Greymist Fair, and never came as a surprise. The only surprise was in the *who* and the *how*. Expressions turned grim as Ulrich described the clothing left behind and where it had been found. About how the signs pointed to a warg attack. All the villagers remembered that day four years ago when beautiful Katrina had died, even if they didn't say it, and their eyes found Heike in the corner of the room. Murmurs grew louder and louder, until Ulrich finished speaking and someone in the back said, "It's got to be the witch, hasn't it? The witch, sending her wargs out."

"We don't know what did this," Ulrich said.

Someone else called out, "But the wargs killed Hilda and Katrina, and they died the same way, and the witch controls the wargs."

"It could be the wargs, yes, but the wargs never leave blood," Ulrich said.

The villagers' voices rose and rose until they nearly drowned him out. "The witch killed Hilda when Hilda was of no use to her anymore," Jürgen yelled, "and she killed Katrina because she was Lord Greymist's daughter, and now she's come for the rest of us."

Several people looked toward the windows of the great room as if the witch would appear then and there to gut them. Heike balled her fists in her skirts. If the witch came after anyone, it would be Heike herself. She looked like her mother, she wore her mother's clothes, she practiced her mother's profession. A cold stone of guilt settled in her stomach. The one thing her mother had never taught her was how to go into the forest and speak to the witch. She'd never said where the witch lived or what the witch looked like. She'd never told Heike how to keep the witch and her wargs away from the village.

Did she tell me and I didn't listen? Heike thought, pressing herself into the corner. *Was that her real task, and her tailoring allowed her to stay in the village? Should I have been speaking to the witch in her absence? And because I haven't, can the wargs now attack us on the road . . . ?*

Ulrich took a step back and raised his hands. His voice boomed across the inn. "Everyone, listen. We *don't know* if the witch or the wargs did this. What we need to do now is decide what measures to take to keep ourselves and our families safe."

Heike heard him because she was standing so close, but other voices had already begun to call out over his.

"We should find where she rests and burn it."

"But we can't go into the woods."

"If enough of us go, we can. She can't kill all of us."

"When?"

"Immediately."

"It's already too dark."

"First thing in the morning. As soon as the sun is high enough to brighten the forest."

"What if she kills some of us?"

"That's why we'll take volunteers. We all know what we're heading toward."

"Who's volunteering, then?"

Heads turned. They looked at Ulrich, at Gottfried, at Dagny and Falk. They looked at those who sometimes went into the woods or who might be brave enough to go now. Falk the fisherman, with his battered and fur-lined coat and his gray hair curling around his ears, made no move from where he stood with his son, but his watery eyes darted from face to face. Gottfried, who was kneeling near the front and scratching The Duke between the ears, said, "It's not much of a plan, is it?"

The room went quiet. Heike's stomach turned, guilt and responsibility and her mother's warning frothing together. Her head felt light, her feet heavy. The firelight swam around her. Wenzel stood on the opposite side of Ulrich's table, and when Heike stepped forward, the color fled his face. Ulrich saw her. Then the others.

"I could go," she said. "I could go alone to speak to the witch."

The flames crackled merrily in the silence.

Wenzel said, "No," at the same time Hans said, "Why would she listen to you?"

"My mother spoke to her," Heike went on, ignoring them both. "She didn't tell me how or where, but she kept the witch away for many years. I could try. She might listen to me. She might."

"What if you're under her control?" Jürgen said. "Your mother might have been."

"Why not let her go?" asked Elma Klein, the farmer. "She's got the best chance of any of us."

"Heike can't go alone," said Wenzel. "None of you would go alone. None of you would send your children, either."

A watery feeling gathered around Heike's knees, so she kept her eyes on Wenzel instead of the crowd before her. "They aren't sending me. I'm sending myself."

"Jürgen's right," called someone in the crowd. "This could be a ploy by the witch."

Heike looked into the crowd but couldn't see who had spoken. The faces that looked back at her were scared, uncertain. She said, "No one controlled my mother, and no one controls me. Tomorrow morning I'll go into the woods to find the witch, and if I don't return by nightfall, you can send your party after her."

More mutters stirred the room, but she only caught one firm disagreement, and after Wenzel uttered it, he covered his eyes with his hand and leaned back against the wall. Ulrich kneeled down, hand on Heike's shoulder, and said, "I don't like the idea of sending you in by yourself. Is this what you want to do?"

"Yes."

"You're absolutely sure?"

"I don't want anyone else to get hurt. I'll be alert. I'll be quick."

Ulrich nodded and stood. "All in favor of Heike's plan raise your hand."

Several went up right away. Jürgen's. Elma's. Then Johanna, Norbert, Falk. Oswald raised his hand, then elbowed Gottfried hard in the ribs, to which Gottfried jammed his hands stubbornly in his armpits. He was joined by Wenzel, still covering his eyes; Ulrich, glancing at Gabi where she stood by Liesel; Gabi, who looked like she might set fire to those who had already agreed; and Doctor Death, whose tired gaze met Heike's across the room and quickly looked away. Ulrich began to count the hands under his breath, then stopped. "I suppose we're for it, then."

four

The next morning Heike took the yarn from the pot over the long-dead fire and hung it up to dry. It had taken on the deep blood red of the berries, her mother's favorite color, and it would be some time before she could make anything of it. She arranged the strands flat and straight and allowed herself a few moments to watch the dark water drip and pool on the floor.

Only a few villagers came to see her off. They stood by the back of the inn while Wenzel packed and repacked bread, cheese, and a waterskin in Heike's bag. Ulrich had come with him and stood facing the forest.

"The trees will turn you around," he said. "The forest wants us to get lost. I've tried marking my trail with sticks, with rocks, with yarn. The sticks get knocked down, the rocks buried, the yarn torn from the branches. I once tried to tie a line from one tree to the next as I went deeper in, and on my way back I found the line cut and scattered on the forest floor."

"Did you ever see what did it?"

"No. I'm not sure it was one creature. It may have been many." He took a small knife from his belt and held it out to her. "Take this. Falk discovered that it can't get rid of cuts on the trees. It tries to slash them out, but that's still a mark. At least you'll keep yourself on one path."

Heike started to tuck the knife into her belt, then thought better of it and kept it in her hand. Wenzel yanked the flap of her bag down over its lumpy contents and frowned at her boots.

"Your hair needs cutting," she said. "We'll do that when I get back."

He grunted.

Doctor Death appeared around the side of the inn. He glanced once at the group of villagers before passing them by. Under the gray morning light, Doctor Death looked carved from bone. The collar of his black coat curved up around his jaw, and its tails flapped around his legs. As he approached, his colorless eyes roved from Heike to Ulrich to Wenzel and back again. His high cheeks and beaked nose had turned red in the chilly air.

"Something wrong, Doctor?" asked Ulrich.

Doctor Death stopped several feet away. He was always accompanied by a shift in the air, an unease that reminded Heike of the feeling she got when she discovered a dead bird splayed on the ground. It was the feeling that kept the villagers away from him unless a loved one was mortally ill. Early winter frost had gathered around his boots, though the ground nearby showed no sign of it.

"Head northwest," the doctor said. "If you reach the bend of the Idle River, you've gone too far."

"You know where the house is?" Heike said.

Doctor Death reached into his coat and pulled out a small leather pouch. He unwrapped the cord from around the pouch, folded it open, and drew out a dried sprig of plant.

"Keep this with you," he said. "In a pocket where it won't fall out. Not in your bag. You might lose that."

Heike took it from him. "Sage? My mother always tied this to our door."

"It will act as a ward. Or I hope it might. Keep it with you."

She tucked the sprig of sage in the deep pocket she'd sewn into her skirts. "Thank you."

"Safe journey," he said, studying her. "Your mother prepared you well."

He turned then and walked away. Heike, Wenzel, and Ulrich watched him go. The spot where he'd been standing was free of frost, the grass a soft green-yellow.

"Do you think that's safe?" Wenzel asked. "What he just gave you? Is it really sage?"

"The doctor has no reason to put any of us in danger," said Ulrich. "Heike, you should leave now before it gets any later."

Heike waited until Doctor Death's tall form disappeared around the inn again, then drew Wenzel into a hug. He hugged her back tightly without hesitation. As she pulled away, she kissed his cheek and said, "I'll return before nightfall. There's plenty to do here, so I'll be upset if I find you waiting."

Wenzel pressed his lips together. Heike looked to Ulrich, who nodded, and then shifted her bag over her shoulder, gripped the knife in her hand, and started toward the forest.

This morning, the trees were still. Their highest branches did not flutter, and the spaces between the trunks were wide and empty and mostly clear of underbrush. Heike oriented herself northwest and used the knife to carve an arrow pointing back toward Greymist Fair on the first tree. Her boots crushed twigs and fallen leaves. On the next tree, she carved another arrow, this one pointing to the first tree. She looked back at Wenzel and Ulrich still watching her, now small enough to pinch between her fingers. She turned around and kept walking. The trees enfolded her.

Heike kept her eyes forward and carved arrows on every tree she passed. Her mother had walked this way often—Heike's own boots had walked this path. The roots of the trees rose from the ground in great arcs and swells as the landscape became an undulating wash of hills and valleys. The muted forest light changed only slightly as the day wore on, growing brighter, then warmer.

Heike stopped only once to eat, nestled between the roots of a tall poplar growing on a slope. As she pulled out the bread and cheese Wenzel had given her, a hard and quick scratching echoed through the woods. The birds had gone quiet overhead. The scratching stopped, then started again, louder, closer. Like claws tearing through tree bark. Stopped, then started, louder again. She stared at the last tree she'd marked, on the opposite side of the small valley, where her small carved arrow was barely visible. The scratching stopped. Heike shoved the cheese into her mouth and the bread into her bag and started walking again.

She carved her arrows faster now, three lines, nine quick strokes to make the cuts deep. The scratching began again behind her. When she turned, there was no sign of any person or animal. She'd seen no other life since she'd entered the woods, though from her cottage she'd spotted rabbits, squirrels, and even the occasional lynx prowling through the trees. She knew there were deer and bears as well, though the only bears she'd seen were the ones Gottfried killed and dragged back to the village.

When she dared to glance behind her, the woods were still and silent, as if patiently waiting for her to continue. She pushed the memory of Tomas's body away and instead thought about her mother. Heike had watched every time her mother had made her new clothes when she was growing up, until they were the same size, and her mother had passed on her bright skirts and the boots that never seemed to wear.

"Never go out without these," her mother had said as she kneeled before Heike and tied the laces, though Heike was well old enough to tie them herself. Her mother had said it with a smile, but there had been a grim set to her mouth as she pulled on an older, dusty pair of boots Heike's grandmother had worn, the laces frayed and the soles peeling. Her mother had always looked grim when she thought Heike couldn't see, and it had aged her beautiful face. In the early mornings, when she'd stood by the twisting trunk of the linden tree and looked down on Greymist Fair, speaking a prayer Heike never heard, she'd appeared as old as the earth. Heike had always wondered if her mother had a magic of her own, a counterpoint to the witch's, strong enough to keep the whole village safe.

Heike knew now that the grim expression had come from the treks her mother had taken through the forest, because Heike was sure that she herself was wearing the same expression. She was lonely but not alone, stalked by something that didn't mind if she knew it was there but wouldn't let her see it. She had been walking for so long, she should have come to the Idle River by now, unless it curved much farther west than she thought. Or perhaps the forest had caught her in the same trap it caught all travelers, on an endless path to a destination that didn't want to be found. Perhaps being hard to find was not a characteristic of Greymist Fair. Perhaps the forest was just good at hiding things.

When Heike walked along the road and wanted to return to Greymist Fair, she thought of home. The branches of the linden tapping at the sides of her cottage. Wenzel and warm milk by the fireplace on a cold evening. The colorful caravans of the traveling merchants who came from faraway lands once or twice a year to set up stalls and trade in the village square. Then the road would fall away behind her and the village would appear between the trees as if she had summoned it.

But that wouldn't work with the witch's home. She didn't know what it looked like, or smelled like, or sounded like. She had no memories there. Heike looked down at her boots and imagined her mother walking this way. She imagined her stepping over fallen branches and through bramble thickets, pushing the sweaty hair from her brow as she trudged on. Her mother had known exactly where the witch lived. She had gone often.

Heike carved her arrow on one more tree, ignoring the frantic scratching that started up several trees behind her, and stepped around the tree and into a clearing.

The forest made a wide and perfect circle around a little cottage with herbs tied to the front door and an ancient linden standing guard.

five

That the cottage was identical to her own startled Heike for only a moment. She approached the door and touched the tied bundle of chamomile, sage, and holly, so similar to the bundle she'd put up on her own door only days ago. The herbs were real, as was the door and the linden tree. When she pushed the door open, it creaked the same way, skidding against the floor before clearing the boards. Heike stepped up and paused in the doorway. An illusion, even a very good one, wouldn't scare her away now.

There was no worktable, no pots of distaffs and spindles. No scattered array of tools, yarns, and fabrics. No dyed wool. Ash covered the hearth, and a thick layer of dust coated the entire room. But there was the same tall, upright loom, as if someone had forgotten to take it with them when they had moved on. Dust motes spun through the air.

On the opposite side of the room, standing before the loom, a person watched the door. They stood very still, as if they had been there for a very long time waiting for her. This person appeared as neither man nor woman. They were very tall, taller even than the doctor, with skin white as snow and hair black as pitch. Their eyes were water under moonlight. A circlet of antlers and thorns rested upon their brow. A heavy wolf pelt curled around their shoulders, its empty and eyeless head nestled by their chin. Beneath, they wore robes that matched the shadows of the room and undulated like smoke. When Heike looked at them, she had the feeling of looking at a dead bird splayed on the ground. Then she had the feeling of watching the bird's feathers rot away, watching the bugs eat its flesh, watching its skeleton crumble into dust. Grass and wildflowers erupted where the bird had once been.

Their black eyes looked her up and down. Their nostrils flared. "You are not the same. You look it, but you are different from her."

"You aren't the witch," Heike said. Her breath sent a flurry of motes into a whirlwind. She kept her hand on the doorframe.

"I am Death," they said.

"Hello," Heike said, because her mother had taught her to be polite to those who had not proven to be dangerous. "Is this the witch's home?"

"This is *my* home," Death said. "Many years ago the witch

tried to steal my family from me. She called me selfish."

Heike cleared her throat. "I'm sorry."

Death's cloak of shadows writhed across the floor, and where the wisps of black smoke went, Death followed, as if tugged along. They stopped in the middle of the room.

"Is it selfish to desire family?" Death asked. "Is it selfish to fear loneliness?"

"No."

"She was a clever witch. She knew how to keep me away." Death looked around again, frowning and waving a pale hand through the air. "She crafted boots that made her swift, so swift I could not catch her."

Heike suddenly felt like she'd spent her whole life looking at the world with one eye closed. She held herself very still.

"She said I never would," Death continued. "She said I would never harm anyone in her village. I said she was temporary, and I am forever. I told her my wargs would keep taking any who feared me in the forest. She stopped wearing her boots, and I caught her. I knew, eventually, you would come here looking for her. I told her I would catch you, too. I would catch you when you entered this place."

"I have not entered," Heike said. Blood beat hard in her cheeks. "You cannot take me."

Death looked at Heike's feet and frowned. Shadows unfurled toward the door. "Your boots," they said. "She gave you her boots."

Heike turned and ran. A blast of winter cold exploded from the cottage and the trees encircling the clearing dropped the last of their leaves all at once. Frost cracked across the grass. Claws tore at her bag and ripped the strap, spilling her food and waterskin. She stumbled and sprinted into the trees.

Shadows raced past her, licking at her heels, tugging at her skirts, catching on her braid. Her ribbon fluttered away and her hair came loose in strands of copper and gold. She looked for her arrows, but there were now only vicious gouges in the trunks.

Death flew, but Heike flew faster. The hills and valleys that had taken hours to traverse now disappeared beneath the boots her mother had given her. Hulking black shapes charged between the trees to her left and right. Death's voice was a gentle brush against her ear. They said, *Do not be afraid.*

Heike thought, *I am afraid. My mother was afraid, too. We are all afraid.*

She thought about Greymist Fair. She thought about being very little and peering into the depths of the well in the center of the village. She thought about the bright streamers and the smells of spiced meat cooking over the caravan fires. Ulrich making her a wooden doll with horse's hair when Liesel broke her little toy dog. Learning to dance the ländler with Wenzel in front of the fire in the great room of the inn, with the tables and chairs pushed against the walls. Long naps beneath the bent trunk of the linden tree. Watching her mother work, listening to her mother's instructions, making her own clothes that wore out slower than they should have and never lost their color. Her mother, standing on the hill against the dawn, not praying.

All at once the trees bowed backward and the forest spit Heike into the cold night. She stumbled as time whipped forward and caught up with her. Her eyes struggled to adjust to the darkness. Greymist Fair was a sprinkling of lantern lights before her, all the way from Ulrich's cottage in the north to the Klein farm in the south. She kept racing toward the inn, where a light shone in every window on both floors, and when she passed the bottom of the hill where her own cottage stood, she saw him emerge from the inn and charge toward her.

"Inside!" she yelled. "Get inside!"

Wenzel skidded to a stop just before they collided, changed course, and they ran together into the inn. Heike shoved the heavy door shut and peered out through a window.

The forest was still. The darkness between the trees was only the darkness of the night. She huffed out the last of her breath and turned to Wenzel, who stood in the small space between the door and the wall with the lamp light creating deep shadows on his face.

"My mother," Heike panted. "My mother was the witch."

Wenzel grabbed her arm and pulled her into an embrace. They fell hard against the wall, rattling the lamp on its table. And just as time had caught up with her, so did her own fatigue, and she felt like all the bones had slid from her body and her muscles had turned to water.

"Ulrich and some of the others are waiting in the great room," Wenzel said. His stubble scratched her temple, and she reached up to hold his head in place so she could rub her cheek against his.

Her mother was the witch. Her mother was the witch. She had loved Greymist Fair more than anything except Heike herself, and she had spent her life protecting it. Again, Heike got the overwhelming feeling that she had been looking at the world with one eye closed, and now both were open. Her mother had taught her everything she knew. But had Heike known what *everything* meant? Could she see it now?

When the feeling returned to her legs, she stood on her own and said, "Don't tell anyone."

They went to the great room, where Ulrich, Gabi, and Liesel

waited at a table by the fire. Heike startled when she noticed Doctor Death standing in the corner behind them, his clothes blending with the shadows and his head high enough to be a trophy on the wall.

Ulrich and Gabi pushed back from the table and stood, relief on their faces.

"The witch is dead," Heike said. "I found her home in the woods. Death was there, and they said they killed her years ago. They control the wargs. They tried to kill me, too, but I ran."

Gabi came forward to inspect her. "Are you okay?"

"Yes."

"Did you discover what killed Tomas?" Liesel asked.

"As soon as I marked the trees, the marks were scratched out by something I didn't see, like Ulrich said they would be. It sounded like claws raking on the bark. When I ran back, something helped Death chase me. I didn't see what it was."

"The wargs," said Liesel.

Heike didn't answer, though she knew Liesel was right. She didn't want to think of those shadows again.

"We'll alert the rest of the village," Ulrich said. "The hunting party won't go out in the morning. If Death itself took Tomas, the best we can do is stay out of the forest, as we've always done."

Heike didn't think doing as they'd always done was the answer, but she didn't know what the answer was, so she let them file out and return to their own homes. She slept in the inn that night so she didn't have to go back to her cottage, her dreams filled with images of her mother speaking to her, though she couldn't hear the words. The next morning she ventured out to climb her hill before the sun rose. She stood beneath the linden tree as light broke over their valley. The shepherd's flock roved like a butter-white cloud across the north field. Gottfried strolled toward the center of the village with his gun on his shoulder and The Duke loping beside him. Wenzel was singing as he pruned the roses that climbed the walls of the inn.

Heike took Doctor Death's sprig of sage from her pocket, considered it for a moment, then put it back and patted it flat. She looked out over Greymist Fair. Her mother had stood here once, not praying, but casting magic of her own. Magic that had been stronger than Death. She had taught Heike everything she knew.

Maybe she had taught her some magic, too.

THE
PRINCE'S
RIDDLE

one

The only thing the prince loved more than himself was magic.

He loved the instantaneousness of it, how one moment it didn't exist and the next it did. He loved how many forms it took, from curses to transformations to enchantments, all beautiful in their own ways. But most of all he loved the reactions of others to magic, and the wonder that overtook them when he granted their wish.

He had two great sadnesses in life. The first was that his only magic was wish granting. The second was that he could not grant wishes for himself.

The prince worried his magic would run out, so he granted wishes only to those who could answer a riddle, and he changed the riddle depending on whether he wanted the person to be able to guess it. Nonsense riddles stumped the nobles of the court, who thought they could wring magic out of him for their enjoyment; easy riddles allowed commoners in the market to win. He didn't mind letting the commoners win. They had true joy on their faces when he granted their wishes, and they never asked for anything outrageous. A bigger house. A stronger horse. A cured illness. He never let children play. Children always wanted the sky a different color or their friend turned into a donkey.

The prince did not intend to go to jail for turning a child into a donkey.

"Couldn't you twist it somehow?" the prince's companion, Evren, asked one day after the prince turned a group of children away. "You know, get them to say, 'Turn my friend *to* a donkey,' and then the magic just spins them in the direction of the nearest donkey?"

"There's not much time between the wishing and the granting," the prince said dryly. What he didn't want to admit was that there was *no* time between the two. It seemed that by imposing his riddle rule, he had inadvertently given up part of his control. If someone answered a riddle correctly, the prince *had* to grant the wish, but he couldn't choose the time or the place or the interpretation. It was like the riddles sucked the magic out of him. And, since he'd started asking riddles, he could no longer grant wishes *without* asking riddles.

Three great sadnesses.

Soon the prince grew tired of his court and his people grew used to his magic, and he felt stifled and hot and sad on his throne, so he took Evren and they set off to travel the world. When he granted wishes, he selected his target very carefully: a person who needed help, who was desperate for it, and who had enough sense to answer an easy riddle.

One day he met an old woman in the desert whose well had run dry. He made the riddle about the sun, the thing she baked under every day. When he left, the woman, standing next to a deep freshwater pool in a lush oasis, waved him off with a big smile.

In the mountains, a married couple couldn't conceive. They had tried for years and suffered several miscarriages. The answer to the prince's riddle was their front door, bright red against the emerald green of the hills and the snowy white of the peaks. The wife wished to be pregnant, and the prince's magic—which seemed to know exactly what the wish maker meant, even when the prince himself didn't—made her stomach swell nearly to bursting. There was a moment of panic among all of them, but the baby was delivered safely, right there on the doorstep.

The prince and his companion moved to cooler climates, through vineyards and valleys, along steep mountain passes and through cities that looked nothing like the prince's homeland. On the outskirts of one such city, they joined a caravan traveling east. The caravan leader, a woman named Jocasta who had a craggy face and a big smile, said she liked the prince's sass and his stories, and he might help bring in some revenue.

The caravan was all performers and craftspeople: musicians, actors, artists, woodworkers. They hailed from all over, not more than two of them from the same region. They set up shop in villages, towns, and cities to trade their wares and entertainment for coin and goods. They had established circuits, and they traveled those circuits several times a year, weather permitting.

"We're headed into the forest now," said Omar, one of the musicians, while the prince watched him harness the horses to his cart. "You said you like magic? You'll like the forest, then. There is a different world inside the woods, and in that world is a village that breathes magic."

Breathes magic sounded exactly like the kind of thing one might say if one did not see magic performed often, thought the prince, but he acted politely intrigued anyway. He'd never been to this forest or the village inside it, and doubtless there would be plenty of people there he could show some *real* magic to.

"The village is called Greymist Fair," said Omar, pulling a strap tight and then looking around, as if he'd misplaced something. "It's not much to look at, but the villagers have quality goods and are happy to trade for the entertainment"—he paused here to shout at the top of his lungs—*"ILYAS! WHAT HAVE I TOLD YOU ABOUT YOUR LAZINESS—"*

On the grassy slope behind the prince, a small boy with a tattered book was huddled behind a tree trunk. When his father began to yell, he leaped to his feet, the book behind his back, his face a mask of terror. He was a cute child, Ilyas, smooth brown skin and big dark eyes, but in the short time the prince had traveled with the caravan, he had known the boy to do little more than daydream and cry.

"Oh, not again," groaned Evren as Omar stormed over to his son, ripped the book from his hands, and dragged him to the cart. The sound of a belt whipping and a small child's cries were heard shortly after. "Horrible man," spat Evren. "The boy doesn't deserve that."

And we don't deserve to listen to the boy crying for hours, either, the prince thought, but Evren would reprimand him for it, so he kept it to himself.

Ilyas *did* cry for hours afterward, a muted snuffling from the back of the cart that had the prince wanting to whip Ilyas himself.

"Can't you just . . ." Evren made a motion with his hand in the air that didn't mimic anything but clearly meant *grant him a wish?* "Surely he'd use it well."

"Even if he did—which he *won't,* because children never *do*—" the prince said, "he's too scared of me to answer any riddles I pose him."

"Then keep asking him until he gets it right," Evren said.

"No."

"Altan."

The prince shot Evren a look. Evren bowed his head. "Sorry. My prince."

"Look, he's fallen asleep," the prince said. He didn't know for sure that the boy was sleeping, but his small form wasn't moving and he was quiet at last. "He'll be fine. Once he learns to listen to his father, he won't have any trouble."

Evren turned away, lips pursed in displeasure and disagreement. He, too, knew when not to say something that would incite an argument.

The forest was dark and dense, and if not for Evren's pocket watch, they would have lost track of the time of day. There was no sun here, only the ghostly light that filtered between the trees and the bluebell flames in iron lamps along the cobbled road. Owl cries haunted the deep forest. The far darkness was tinted the purple-blue of bruises. Jocasta had warned them before they set out not to leave the road for anything, no matter what they saw or heard. The prince's skin prickled beneath his shirt and brocade jacket, a telltale sign of ambient magic.

Evren's watch stopped working after they passed over a worn stone bridge and a swift river Jocasta called the Idle without a trace of irony in her voice. After that they had no notion of how long the journey took. The prince thought three hours; Evren said five. Omar claimed the time could not be measured here. Many in the caravan had tried keeping track of the seconds, but all counts were wildly different. The forest denied them any ability to know how far they had gone or how much farther they had to go. They would arrive when it wanted them to arrive.

At last the trees parted to reveal a gentle slope down into a village of stone and thatch cottages. The sky overhead was overcast, as if the sun had only just now dipped below the fat, dark clouds on the horizon. The caravan passed through silent farmland and into the center of the village, where the buildings were larger and shingled. They were followed by a gaggle of children and adults, the children squealing in excitement and the adults beaming, waving, excited in their own way. The prince had expected less from the village. Peasants, first of all, in rough-spun clothing with dirty faces and bad teeth. In reality, the villagers' clothes were quite fine, they were clean, and the smiles he could see were better than his own. Despite the overcast skies, the mood was anything but gloomy. Perhaps this was how they lived.

And if the forest had felt like an untamed, gloom-flashing magic, the buildings, the people, and the very blades of grass of Greymist Fair all formed a complex living web of magic that made the prince's hair stand on end. Magic vibrated in his heart like a tuning fork.

He loved it.

two

Greymist Fair had one inn, the largest of all the buildings save for the manor house on the eastern rise. The inn was three stories of stone and wood, one side grown over with wine-red roses, and it was run by a sweet elderly couple for whom the prince dearly wanted to grant a wish or two.

"A wish?" said the woman, blinking her watery eyes behind the thick lenses of her eyeglasses. "Oh, my dear, I don't need any wishes at my age. I've got all I want."

"Nothing?" the prince said. "I don't see any grandchildren. What about a little one you can spoil to your heart's content?"

"And who would take care of the poor thing after we were gone? Quite a terrible idea, to bring about a child with the knowledge that you'll abandon it."

"Ask for youth, then," suggested the prince. "Who wouldn't want to be young again?"

She laughed. "My mother used to say youth is for the young. When you're my age, you're too cautious to put that body to good use."

"Surely, though, it could help with the pains?" asked the prince. "Your eyes, even? Wouldn't you like to be able to see well again?"

"I've never seen well," the woman said patiently. "And pains—well, *my* pains, anyway—are symbols of a life well lived. They are part of me now, like the color of my hair or the shape of my fingers. Maybe if they were caused by some disease, or if they were unbearable, or if I was going to die before my time . . . But no, my dear, my pains are mine, and I've come to terms with them." She laughed. "Besides, the tinctures Luther gives me work perfectly well. He's quite a good doctor."

"But . . . dying . . ." the prince continued weakly.

She patted his arm. "We all face death in the end. It's nothing to be afraid of."

The prince couldn't think of anything to say. If he could wish himself free of death, he'd have done it long ago.

"If she doesn't take one, I'm afraid I can't, either." The woman's husband, sweeping the inn's front steps, winked at her. "Can't let her take all the glory, can I? Besides, I'm not all that good at riddles."

The prince was baffled. No one had ever refused him before; they had all at least *tried* the riddle.

The caravan settled in the grassy field behind the inn. Many of the others in the caravan chose to stay in rooms at the inn, accepting the innkeepers' hospitality in exchange for a week's worth of entertainment, several brand-new, very expensive rugs, and a chest full of spices from distant lands. Others chose to sleep in their carts and wagons, citing habit rather than the obvious aim of theft prevention.

That very night the theatrical and musical performers set up a show in the square that drew the entire village. The story was about a woman whose children were all eaten by a wolf. While the wolf slept off his meal, the woman cut him open, freeing the children from his stomach, and replacing them with stones. The wolf died at the end, of course—there were children in the audience, so the troupe wasn't going to perform any sad endings tonight—but the prince still thought it was a bit of a grim story for the occasion.

Yet not one of the villagers seemed to mind. If anything, they cheered harder than he expected when the wolf fell to his death.

"Understanding your audience is the key to a good performance," Jocasta said, a twinkle in her eye. "Even the babes here understand and fear death. They always like to see it defeated."

The prince wasn't sure that was the reason they cheered, though. Death *wasn't* defeated; it was only fed a different victim.

The prince, standing on the edge of the crowd with Evren, spent much of the time scanning the audience, watching faces the way he did when he performed magic. The villagers' reactions were surprisingly similar: anticipation, a little worry, then shock, wonder, joy.

"Don't sulk," Evren said, reading the prince's mind in his magicless way. "If you want to be the one who gives them these feelings, why don't you volunteer to help with the show?"

But the prince's problem wasn't just that *he* wanted to be the one to give them joy; he wanted *magic* to be what gave them joy. He wanted everyone else to love it as much as he did.

A face in the crowd caught the prince's eye. She was young and beautiful and had a small girl on her lap who looked very much like her. A little sister, perhaps? The young woman's long gold-brown hair was gathered to one side of her neck and tied with a red ribbon, and blood-red skirts fanned on the ground around her. There were splotches of color throughout the audience, illuminated by the lamps and torches, but she was the brightest of them. She seemed to be enjoying the show, but not wholly engrossed in it, the way others were. *She* would be one to really appreciate magic.

The prince waited until the performance ended and the crowd rose to disperse, then cut through the gathering to where the woman had been sitting. When he got there, though, she and the little girl were gone.

"Who was the woman in the red skirts?" the prince asked the innkeepers later that night.

The old man, carrying three mugs and a set of grease-smeared plates back to the kitchen, stopped and thought for a moment. "You mean Hilda? Some of the other girls have gotten the idea in their heads to wear bright colors, but she's the only one with red skirts, far as I know."

"She had a small child with her. A girl that looked like her. Big eyes, gold hair."

"That's Hilda, dear," called the old woman from the hearth, where she was rearranging chairs.

"That's Hilda, then," said the man. "Sweet lass. Keeps to herself much of the time, especially since her mother died. Travels into the forest to speak with the witch, keep her happy and away from the Fair. She's the finest tailor in town, if you need something made or mended."

"And the little girl, that's her sister?"

"Oh no, her daughter. Little Henrike."

"She's married?"

"No, no, not that I know. And you don't get married in Greymist Fair without the whole village knowing."

Unmarried and with a child. Even better. He had never met a person with a child who didn't want a companion to make them whole.

The old innkeeper narrowed his eyes good-naturedly at the prince and wagged the index finger not preoccupied with a heavy mug. "Now there, you aren't crafting some scheme to steal young Hilda away, are you?"

"Of course not," said the prince with a happy smile. "I would never."

He wouldn't have to. She would wish for him.

three

Hilda the tailor lived in a cottage on a hill bordering the forest. The prince could see it from his room, small in the distance and half-hidden by the branches of a towering linden tree. A light burned in a tiny window.

The next day the prince gathered one of his brocade coats and several shirts that had become frayed and torn through the course of his travels, with the intent to ask the tailor to mend them. Evren was to come with him, but when Evren emerged from the inn, he was toting Ilyas. The boy had been crying recently—it was rare when he did *not* cry—and hid himself behind Evren's legs as he let himself be led forward.

The prince glanced down at him pointedly.

"I know," Evren said, "but I wasn't going to let his father whip him again just for looking at roses. He won't get in your way."

The prince doubted that, but turned and marched up the hill without arguing.

The little girl, Henrike, was playing with a doll of sticks beneath the linden tree. She watched them as they approached the cottage, her gaze quickly finding Ilyas and sticking to him. She was like a small lion, wary golden eyes and a posture that suggested a new hunt. A dried bundle of herbs hung from the cottage door. The sun was peeking out between the clouds, casting a watery yellow glow against the warped panes of glass in the window.

Before the prince could knock, Henrike called out in a high, bell-chime voice, "*Mama!*"

The door swung open. Hilda appeared before them, brushing hair from her eyes, looking surprised. Behind her stood a large loom, hung with thread. Hilda looked quickly toward Henrike as if to make sure her call hadn't been for anything more serious, then turned back to the prince.

"Good morning," she said. She gave a brisk nod. "Can I help you with anything?"

The prince introduced himself and Evren, then held up his stack of clothing. "I was told you were the best tailor in the village. I was hoping I could employ your services."

Henrike had scampered over from the tree, but instead of standing beside her mother, she went straight for Ilyas. She held out her stick doll for him and, after enough prompting, he carefully took it.

Hilda watched them. "Yours?" she asked, motioning to Ilyas.

"No," the prince replied quickly. "He's with the caravan. Evren is looking after him for now."

Evren had knelt down with the two children and was facilitating play. Ilyas's tears had dried and he was smiling as he cast furtive glances at Henrike. Perhaps the prince had been wrong, then—the boy wouldn't get in his way.

"Could we step inside?" the prince asked Hilda, motioning past her. "I can show you what I need."

"Oh—of course," she said.

The inside of the cottage was cramped with tools and other odds and ends the prince assumed were for tailoring. His eyes passed over the details and saw the larger picture. One room, not very large and cluttered besides, a single bed for both mother and child. It got better and better. What *wouldn't* she wish for? Beauty and youth, he supposed—she had plenty of both, at least for now.

"The clothing?" she said, pulling him from his thoughts. Her gaze had sharpened since he'd come in; her eyes were honey gold in the shaft of sunlight entering through the open door.

He took her through the wear on each article of clothing, watching her face change as he spoke, watching her hands move over the material. She was calm and confident in her craft as she explained to him how she would mend the damage. He didn't listen to her—he didn't care how or even if the clothes were mended—but he enjoyed watching her mouth.

"I'm in your debt," he said when she had finished. "Truly. I can pay you in coin, or I could perhaps bring some fabrics or other items from the caravan for you, if that would be more useful. Or . . . well, I have another method of payment that many people prefer, but it would require you to do one small thing."

"I'm not interested in that," she said plainly, shoulders stiff.

"Oh no!" The prince raised his hands. "No, my lady, I apologize; I didn't mean to imply anything impure. Rather, what I meant was that I can pay you with a wish. I can grant wishes, you see. All you must do is answer a simple riddle, nothing that would be too hard for you to handle, I'm sure, and the wish is yours. Whatever you'd like."

Her shoulders relaxed and her eyebrows lifted. "Magic? I see. Yes, that's certainly not so impure. Anything I like, you say?"

"Whatever your heart desires."

Her gaze skimmed toward the open door, through which Henrike and Ilyas were visible. They were chasing each other around the base of the linden tree under Evren's watchful eye. "Mmm. Why a riddle? Have you been cursed?"

The prince shifted as her sharp attention returned to him.

She wasn't surprised when confronted with magic, or if she was, she recovered very quickly. And she apparently wasn't as easily dazzled by the promise of it as some people were. The same was true with the innkeepers.

"No curses," he explained. "I have always had magic. The riddles were my own fault; one day I started awarding wishes for correctly answered riddles, and that was what my magic became."

She studied him, seemed to catalogue the parts of him. "Interesting. This riddle, do I have to answer it immediately? Can I hear it now and have some time to think on it, or should I wait until I'm sure I'd like to take the wish, and then I can hear the riddle?"

No one had ever asked the prince such a question. "I suppose you can hear it, though I promise any riddle I give you would be as easy as I could make it. In exchange for your work, of course."

"Oh, of course," she said. A small smile played on her lips. "I'd like to hear the riddle, then. Tell me now, then come back at the end of the week, before the caravan leaves. I'll have all your mending done so you can pick it up and hear the answer."

She had taken the bait *and* she'd given him a week to manipulate her wish. He could easily charm his way close to her by then. He couldn't have planned it better himself.

"One week," the prince said, smiling with all his teeth. "The night before the caravan leaves."

"And the riddle?"

It was his easiest, not because everyone knew the answer, but because it had many answers, and to him they were all correct. It was almost impossible to answer incorrectly.

"What leaves you empty," he said, *"and fills you up?"*

four

Each morning the prince bought a fresh loaf of bread from the bakers across the village square and took it up to Hilda's cottage on the hill. On the third day she caught on and began meeting him halfway down the hill, Henrike in tow. Hilda would oblige him with a stroll around the town square, where Henrike would run off to play with some of the other children or with Ilyas, who had taken to following Evren like a small shadow.

Hilda asked the prince questions about his homeland and his magic, and for the first time the prince found himself explaining his deep love of magic to someone else. He had never done so before, though not for lack of trying; most people seemed to think he loved it because he could do it when no one else could. But Hilda listened, and he sensed that there was an understanding in her—maybe because of something she said, or the way she cocked her head—that he loved magic for what it was.

She wanted to know about all the wishes he'd ever granted, the riddles he'd given, why he'd given them and to whom. How did he choose his recipients? Had he ever tried to have someone he trusted wish that he could have full control of his magic again, without the use of the riddles? He admitted that he hadn't considered that before, but he would now.

He asked her what she would wish for. She said she didn't know. He moved closer as he asked the questions intended to get her thinking. Was she lonely? How long had she been living with her daughter on their hill, separated from the village not only by distance but by her duty to protect the town from the witch in the forest? Did she wish she could live a normal life, a peaceful life? She never answered these questions directly, just made small noises of acknowledgment.

By the sixth day, most of the town seemed to know of the prince's wish-granting abilities. He was certain Hilda hadn't told anyone, so it had either been a stray word from the innkeepers or from a member of the caravan. The prince didn't mind once he realized that the promise of magic didn't entice the villagers to come to him with requests or pleas. They seemed to share the innkeepers' and Hilda's reluctance when it came to magic. Maybe they thought they'd had enough of it.

Well, it didn't entice the *adult* villagers.

That afternoon, long after Hilda had excused herself from their walk to return to her work, the prince was lounging outside the inn, basking in the sunlight, when a small voice accosted him.

"I want a wish."

He looked around and found a waif of a boy, no older or bigger than Hilda or Ilyas, standing several feet away and staring at him with blank blue eyes. The boy's blond hair was weedy and hung in his face.

"I don't grant wishes to children," said the prince. "Go away."

He closed his eyes again, but he felt the boy still standing there, staring at him.

"I want. A wish," the boy said.

"I want. You to go away," replied the prince.

There was a scrape of rock and then a sharp pain across the prince's forehead. He leaped to his feet, wiping blood from a cut above his eye, just in time to dodge another rock. He surged forward, caught the boy's scrawny wrist, and twisted until the boy cried out and dropped the rock.

"Little devil!" the prince snapped, shaking the boy. "This is why I don't grant wishes to children! You're fiendish, impulsive things. You can't be trusted!"

There was a brief, high-pitched scream from across the square. "Hans! Oh, Hans! Take your hands off him, you brute!"

A blond woman came flying over to rip the boy from the prince's grasp. She glared at the prince as she checked little

Hans's wrist and head and the whole rest of his body, as if the toad had been in a brawl.

"How dare you?" she exclaimed, pressing Hans close to her chest. "How dare you handle him like that—he's just a baby!"

Hans's flat blue eyes stared at the prince from the depths of his mother's cleavage. A crowd was beginning to gather on the edges of the square.

"He was throwing rocks at me because I wouldn't grant him a wish," said the prince, jabbing a finger at the cut on his forehead. "Is this what you teach your spawn to do when they don't get their way? Throw rocks?"

"Why couldn't you just give him a wish?" Hans's mother was wailing louder now, as if *she* had been the one hit with a rock. There were actual *tears* in her eyes. "He's a little boy, he only wants a wish, how could you be so cruel to withhold a wish from a *child*?"

Evren appeared by the prince's side then, ready to smooth the situation over, but the prince held up his hand.

"Fine," he said, teeth bared. "Your devil child wants a wish, he has to answer a riddle first. That's how it works, and *everyone* has to do it."

The mother blinked at him as Hans wriggled out of her tight embrace, almost shoving her away. "I can do it," he said. "I can answer riddles."

The prince loomed over him. "Here it is, hellion. *What slew none, and yet slew twelve?*"

The boy was so young he seemed not even to completely understand the form of the question. Even if he had, he couldn't have gotten it right, because this riddle had no answer. The prince had created it intentionally as a riddle with no answer, so no matter what answer was given, it would be wrong. It was the counterpoint to his easiest riddle.

Hans stood silent, his lips pressed tight, his face turning red, his eyes roving around the square.

"That's too hard," complained Hans's mother. "Can't you ask him something easier, so he can answer it? Or so I can answer it for him?"

"You can't answer for him," the prince spat, his ire well and truly up. "*He* must answer, and he gets the riddle that he gets. The world does not hand out wishes on a platter just because one is a *child*, and *your* child is no more special than any other. Oh, did you not realize? Better you find out now than later, I suppose—"

"*Altan!*" Evren hissed in his ear, jerking his arm to pull him away. "That's *enough!*"

The prince turned to the boy once more. "And what will you be, little Hans, when you no longer have your mother to hold you and tell you everything will be okay? Will you still be a devil? Or will your neighbors quash you before—"

"*Enough!*" Evren said again, grabbing the prince by the lapels of his coat and bodily shoving him toward the inn. After the first few steps, the prince allowed himself to be pushed, and once they were inside the inn, he stomped his way up to their shared room on his own. Evren shut the door behind them.

"You just told a small boy you hoped his neighbors would kill him," Evren said, red-faced and out of breath.

"If you haven't noticed," the prince replied, dabbing daintily at his bloodied forehead with his kerchief, "I hate children."

"Yes, but normally you're not so vicious about it! We only have one day left. Can you please not get us attacked by the villagers? I'm worried about the caravan, too—I doubt they'll want to associate with us now. We'll have to find our way out of this forest ourselves."

"Shouldn't be too hard; there's only one road."

"Altan, please . . . maybe we should leave now."

"No! I've got plans."

"What, the conquest of a tailor? Surely you can find someone else in the next town or city we come across."

"I'm not leaving yet."

"You're causing more trouble, is what you're doing."

"Tomorrow is the day she'll let me grant her wish," the prince said. "Tomorrow night, during the troupe's final performance. I'll stay here until then, what about that? I won't leave this room."

Evren eyed him, looking weary and much older than his years. "You'll stay right here? In this small inn room? I've never known you to stay cooped in a *palace*, much less a room half the size of your wardrobe."

The prince put his hand over his heart. "I swear it, Evren. By our holy bond, I swear it."

Evren sighed. Sank onto the end of his bed.

"Fine," he said. "We'll stay."

Then he put his head in his hand and said, "But *please* . . . do not threaten any more children."

five

The prince kept his word and spent his final day in Greymist Fair cooped up in the room, sitting by the window and watching Hilda's cottage on the hill. The trees swayed behind it like dark giants. He tried desperately not to sink into a bad mood—it wouldn't do to meet her later that night with a thundercloud over his head.

She came from the cottage as she did every morning and stopped halfway down the hill, scanning the area. Then, not spotting him coming to meet her, continued toward the village. That prickled his pride, and all because a blond rat had demanded a wish and refused to leave when told no. The prince's lip curled. Hilda's little Henrike wouldn't be that much of a problem on the road, he was sure. She already wouldn't speak to him. Maybe, when he took Hilda home to his own city and the palace, Henrike would find other little friends to play with and he'd never have to see her.

Evren brought the prince bread and stew from the kitchen

below, and the prince ate slowly while he watched out the window.

"You're obsessed," Evren said, but the prince didn't hear him.

Night fell. The troupe set up on the green behind the inn for their final performance, and the village gathered to watch. Only then did the prince descend from his room and sneak outside, edging around the crowd until he found Hilda. She was on the fringes with her daughter as she had been before, except now Evren sat near them with Ilyas. The prince crept closer. Hilda saw him and whispered something to her daughter, who nodded and stayed where she was. Hilda rose and joined the prince in the shadows.

"Let's go to my cottage," she said, motioning up the hill.

He followed her away from the torches and noise of the performance. Atop the hill, the prince looked up and realized the clouds had dissipated here, giving an uninterrupted view of a blanket of stars overhead. The forest whispered, like thousands of people stood just out of view in the darkness, watching them. The prince forced himself not to look. *There's no one there*, he told himself.

Hilda drew him under the linden tree. Anticipation shivered through the prince's fingers.

"The answer to your riddle is many things," she said. "The answers that first came to mind were love, hope, hate, fear, and death. There are others, of course, but I thought five would be enough for you."

"Plenty," he said, stepping closer to her, feeling her soft breath against his jaw, the warmth of her so near. "What do you wish for?"

He was sure she was smiling when she said, "I *am* going to make my wish, but first I want to say some things."

The prince couldn't see her face in the darkness, but he could imagine it: flushed with color, eyes bright, lips parted. As beautiful as any man or woman he'd been with before. Her hand was solid on his forearm. "Anything you like," he said.

"I have been walking with you this week, asking you these questions about yourself and your magic, because I needed to know your true intentions. I'm not a very hard person to please, but I have lived my whole life in a place where magic is a fickle, wild thing, and I don't think it should be used by fickle, wild people."

The prince started. "If you're talking about the boy—Hans—I didn't—"

She squeezed his arm, silencing him. "Hans is a hell-child, spoiled by his mother and abused by his father, and I feel no regret in saying either thing. You were right to turn him down. You went a bit far, but I understand how the situation started."

He relaxed. "So you see I'm careful with my magic."

She said nothing for a moment, and the silence made the prince shiver. Her eyes flashed in the darkness; the prince blinked and they were shadowed again, human.

"*Careful* might apply to someone who had not leashed their magic to riddles."

The prince stood very still, uncomprehending.

"*Careful* might apply to someone who considers the ramifications of his magic beyond the immediate. Someone who wonders what might become of an old woman in a desert who suddenly has a rich oasis around her house, an oasis that might attract all flavors of weary and dangerous travelers to seek its shelter. *Careful* would be the person who considers the emotional toll of an instant pregnancy upon the human body, and the life of a miracle child born in a small village where magic is either revered or taboo."

The prince's shiver had turned into a cold chill. He tried to pull away from Hilda, but she held him fast. Her nails dug into his forearm like claws.

"I understand why you did not give Hans a wish. I could understand if you gave no one a wish ever again. I would support it, even. What I cannot condone is someone with such considerable power doing nothing to help a child."

"Help a . . . you can't mean Ilyas? The caravan boy?"

He couldn't see her face, but he could feel her stare. A horrible feeling crept over him, cold fingers caressing his shoulders and neck, the weight of darkness wrapping like a blanket. "This is ridiculous," he said, suddenly breathless, tearing his arm from her grip and turning back down the hill. "I won't listen to—"

"*I wish*," she said, and he froze as if a great hand had fallen from the heavens and slammed his shoulders, locking him in place. His eyes bulged. His throat worked, but no sound came out of his mouth. A great laugh exploded from the crowd below, watching the performance and unaware of what was happening above.

"I wish," Hilda said again, her breath on his neck, one of her hands on the small of his back, "you would toss yourself into the waters of Grey Lake, turn into a large and ugly fish, and dwell there until the day all your magic runs out."

He did not process her words fully until he was down the hill, marching dutifully southward to parts of the village he had not yet seen, magic puppeteering his body on an unfamiliar path. Weeds snagged his legs but did not stop him. His feet avoided dips and holes. He thrashed against the inescapable hold of magic, his heart pounding so hard in his chest it was a wonder no one else heard it. If he could only call out to Evren— but no, he could never speak while the magic was being wrung from him. Past the single cobbled road with its iron lanterns was a smaller path into the forest, down to a fisherman's hut erected near a small dock at one end of a vast and oily darkness. Clouds coalesced overhead, hiding the stars.

Wind sheared across the lake. He could not see the other side, but he felt that something wandered there in the darkness, an ancient lurking creature waiting to be fed. He strode down the dock, screaming in his mind, praying for someone to see, someone to find him, someone to stop his march. But he was alone.

The prince dove gracefully into the black lake and disappeared.

six

The morning the caravan was set to leave, Evren dressed slowly, waiting for the prince to tromp back from the tailor's cottage in victory. Evren ate breakfast, made sure their things were properly packed, and checked on their horses. The prince still did not appear.

On his way back from the stables, Evren was stopped by Hilda, carrying the prince's mended garments.

"Would you return these to him, please?" she asked, handing the stack over. "I'm sure he won't want to be bothered if he isn't awake yet."

Evren blinked stupidly at her. "He didn't stay with you last night?"

Hilda cocked her head, looking puzzled. "No, of course not. Is he not here?"

Clutching the prince's clothes to his chest, Evren rushed inside to ask if the innkeepers had seen the prince. They had not. Nor had any of the caravan members, who were loath to talk to him because of the prince's outburst against the villagers, or the other villagers, who didn't particularly like him for the same reason. The last person who had seen the prince was Hilda, when they had walked up the hill during last night's performance, but Hilda claimed the same thing each time he asked her: "I refused the wish—and him, I suppose—and told him I was returning to the performance. He wanted to take a walk."

She looked troubled after the fourth time Evren asked the same question, and added, "He might have gone into the forest. I know he doesn't understand this place, and he doesn't have the respect for the forest that we do. Death dwells there. If he went into the trees unprepared, he's gone now."

Evren, who had been sworn to serve the prince from the day he was born, couldn't believe he was gone, and vowed to remain in the town until the prince was found.

The caravan left. Evren remained with the prince's horse and his clothes.

He spent his days searching the village from north to south, walking the line of the forest but never breaching the trees, going so far as the edge of the lake in the south where the craggy fisherman told him only the children came down to the lake.

Evren went out even at night, hoping that something about the darkness might help him trace the prince's steps or understand what his mindset had been that day. Or, if that didn't work, maybe he would come upon some unsavory character who might have been out that night with the prince, might have seen him—might have had something to do with the disappearance.

He found no unsavory characters, but he did find Ilyas.

The boy was huddled by the Klein's pigpen, eating whatever leftovers he could find in the trough, wild-eyed and sickly. He clung to Evren when he realized who Evren was, and after a dunk in the washtub at the inn and a real meal, he explained what had happened.

The night of the performance, his father had taken him into the trees north of the village and told him to wait there while he went back to the caravan. Ilyas had obeyed because he was more scared of his father than the forest. Amidst the trees of the forest, in that timeless eldritch gloom, he waited until the sun came up . . . but he had eventually panicked and ran, he hoped, in the direction of the caravan. He emerged from the forest and rushed into the village to find the caravan long gone. Alone and terrified, he had hidden himself on the Klein's farm—he liked the animals, he said—and had been there since.

His voice was so dull that Evren wasn't sure if he understood what had happened to him, that his father had left him in the forest knowing that the forest would kill him.

"Poor boy," said the innkeepers, doting on Ilyas, putting him in fresh clothes, setting him to work on easy tasks like sweeping the front walk and praising him softly when he performed well.

There was a moment, fleeting, when Evren wondered if the prince had abandoned him, had forgotten about his horse and his clothing and left because Evren had become too needling about what he used his magic for and why. The longer Evren stayed in Greymist Fair and the more he looked at the forest, the less he believed the prince was coming back.

"We can't live our lives waiting," said Hilda one morning, when she caught Evren sitting listlessly outside the inn. Hilda's young face was lined with worry and something like regret. "I am sorry this happened. I'm sorry you're in such pain."

"I only wish I knew what happened to him," Evren said.

It was early fall when Evren left Greymist Fair. The innkeepers and Hilda both warned him of the difficulty of travel on the road once the heavy winter snows fell. He didn't want to wait and take his chances with the weather, nor did he want to spend several more months in the company of neighbors who either pitied or avoided him.

He mounted his horse and looked down at the two kind old innkeepers and little Ilyas, who was already starting to grow into his new clothes. The boy didn't like the name Ilyas, wouldn't let anyone call him by it, and so no one did. "We'll find him a good new one," said the old man, clapping the boy on the shoulder. "Won't we?"

"I hope you do." Evren gathered his collar tighter around his neck; even now in early fall, the weather was cold. "If the prince . . . if you ever hear anything, or know what might have become of him, please send word to the address I left. I know it's not likely, but if he is . . . I wouldn't want him to think I had left him."

"Of course, dear," said the old woman.

They said quick goodbyes, and then Evren turned down the road, not in the direction the caravan had gone, but back the way they had come. The forest swallowed him quickly. In minutes Greymist Fair disappeared behind him. When he emerged at the forest's edge, into long misty foothills with the sound of the ocean in the distance, it was as if Greymist Fair had never existed at all.

WOLF
CHILDREN

one

Liesel's mother died giving birth to Liesel's younger brother, Tomas. Liesel wasn't old enough to remember it, and her father had told her no details, but she'd watched him dig the grave. Her mother's gravestone stood in the field behind their home, surrounded by weeds and wildflowers.

Liesel's father died ten years later, trampled underfoot by one of Elma Klein's stocky plow horses. It had been spooked by a bolt of lightning that cracked a nearby tree in half and set the remains on fire. Liesel saw his caved-in chest and the blood still soaking into the soil. Elma Klein had dug the grave next to Liesel's mother's, and her father's gravestone was smothered in vines.

Now Liesel buried what remained of Tomas—his boots—in the field beside her parents, with her breath clouding the air as she shoveled dirt into the dark hole, and the sky rumbling with thunder. The worn boots disappeared in sections, then all at once. She did not welcome their going, even though they smelled like corpse.

Jürgen had helped her dig the hole in the hard, cold ground. He was the only person who hadn't yet looked at her with pity, and he hadn't spoken while they worked. Before he left, he handed her the shovel and said, "He was a good boy," then he lumbered back to the village with his shoulders hunched and his ruddy face fixed in a perpetual scowl.

It was late in the afternoon when she finally finished. She planted the shovel at the foot of the grave and set off for the village with dirt caked on her hands and her skirts. Greymist Fair bustled with families preparing for the annual winter trim—a last haircut before the cold months truly set in and a signal that Yule festivities were near. A single chair was brought out of each house. Neighbors conversed as husbands and wives took turns cutting each other's hair, then their children's. Siblings took turns as well if they were old enough, or if there were no parents or siblings, friends would do. Hair gathered on the side of the road to be picked at by the wind and birds. Liesel kept her eyes down as she passed Ada Bosch, with her seven children lined up and the youngest sitting in the chair and swinging his legs and nearly ramming his neck into his mother's scissors. One of the children called out to Liesel, so she walked faster. She looked up only when she got to the center of the village, because she was afraid if she didn't, she'd topple headfirst into the well.

Godric, the blacksmith, sat like a boulder outside his forge while his daughter trimmed away his graying hair. Across the square, Johanna the baker snacked on a malformed loaf of bread while her wife, Dagny, carefully snipped bangs across her forehead. Jürgen now stood outside the butcher shop, hacking at Hans's unruly mane until he looked like a boy again.

"Liesel!"

Wenzel perched on a chair in front of the inn, hand raised in greeting. Behind him, Heike drew her scissors back, looking disgruntled. Liesel's hands itched for scissors, for the soft fall of hair. Tomas had never sat still when she cut his hair. Last year she'd considered tying him to the chair.

Heike glanced at her but didn't wave. Ever since she'd come back from the woods, Heike had acted as if she knew something the rest of them didn't. Just like Heike to act superior. So Death had killed the witch and taken up residence in her shack. It didn't matter to Liesel; Tomas was still gone. Liesel ignored them both and made a beeline for the butcher's shop. Jürgen had disappeared inside and left Hans to sweep up the hair. The muted *thump thump* of metal on wood came from the shop behind him.

"Hi," Hans said. His expression was as blank as always as he looked her up and down. "You could use a wash."

Liesel wiped her hands on her skirts, wishing he would at

least smile when he saw her. She had never known Hans to be warm, but he had coveted her, once, when no one else ever had. "Do you have more work to do today?" she asked.

"No. Father lets me go early on trim days," Hans replied. "Fritz and I were going to go to the lake."

Liesel started. "To Grey Lake? You'd go that close to the forest, after what happened?"

Hans shrugged.

She tugged on his sleeve and swished her skirts, doing her best to look enticing while covered in dirt. "Stay here with me, instead."

Hans looked at her hand on his sleeve, at her face, then to the south, in the direction of Grey Lake. Anger burned up Liesel's arms again. How hard was it to decide between an afternoon with her, sneaking into the loft of Albert Schafer's barn to nest in the hay, and an afternoon with gangly, awkward Fritz on the awful muddy shores of Grey Lake? In the last two years, Hans had never refused her, but he came closer and closer every time.

Hans used his broom to nudge at the dirt around the cobblestones. "Maybe tomorrow."

If she'd had anything to throw, she would have thrown it.

"*Fine*," she spat. "Have fun with Fritz and the lake scum."

He didn't even call after her when she stormed away.

The night was bitterly cold. Liesel wanted to keep a candle lit by her bedside, but since Tomas's death she'd been tossing in the night, and she was afraid she'd knock it over and set the house on fire. She stripped Tomas's bed of its blankets and added them to her own, and as she laid there, shivering and listening to the wind howl through the cracks in the walls, she thought about how cold it must be under the ground.

Trying to keep herself from crying—again—had been a complete failure. She was sick of crying, and it had only been a few days since Tomas was found in the woods. She was sick of not knowing why Tomas had gone down the road, what he'd seen or felt or thought just before Death came for him. She was sick of feeling useless, like there was nothing she could have done to save him even if she'd been there.

The front door slammed open with a thunderous *CRACK*. Liesel screamed and froze, her wet cheeks stinging from the chilled wind that whipped through the room. Moonlight barely outlined the doorframe, and the curls of dead grass on the ground outside. The door banged against the wall once, twice, again and again in a steady rhythm that made Liesel's heart hammer in her chest.

She knew that the latch on the door was bad, and that the

wind was strong enough to blow it open, and all she needed to do was close it and shove something heavy in front of it to keep it shut.

She felt that if she went to close the door, something terrible would happen.

She got up to close it.

Where she'd expected some man or beast to be standing on the road, watching her house, there was nothing. The blue ghostlights flickered along the road, as always. She shut the door. The only heavy thing she still owned that might be able to hold it closed in such a wind was Tomas's bed, so she turned to pull it over.

A boy sat on the edge of the bed. He glowed from the inside out as if he'd swallowed one of the roadside lanterns. His shirt was ripped to shreds, and his terrified face was striped with tear tracks. He looked up at her, shaking in the cold, and said, "Liesel, why did you take my blankets?"

Liesel's flesh prickled from the crown of her head to the soles of her feet.

"Tomas?"

"Have you been crying?" he asked.

Liesel stared at the unblemished, luminescent plane of his chest visible through the rags of his shirt. The wind pushed the door into her back.

"Please don't cry. You'll make my blankets all wet, and then they'll be cold, too."

"What are you?" Her voice was swallowed by the wind, but he still heard her.

"What . . . ? Liesel, it's me." Tomas looked hurt. "Why are you being so cruel?"

"Why are you here? What do you want?"

With the next slam of the door against her back, he was standing before her. He hadn't seemed to move except to tip slightly forward, and then he'd faded from one spot and reappeared in the next. His eyes, which had been a dull gray in life, blazed with blue fire. He smelled like the bitter bite of winter.

"I need to tell you something," he said.

And then he was gone.

The room returned to rattling darkness. The wind thumped the door between Liesel's shoulder blades one, two, three times. She sank to the floor in front of it, arms wrapped around her knees, and remained there until morning.

two

A knock roused her after sunrise. Light streamed in the windows and Liesel rubbed sleep from her eyes. She had curled so tightly around herself in front of the door, her arms and legs had gone stiff.

Please let that have been a dream, she thought as she grabbed the door handle to pull herself to her feet. The knock came again.

Heike stood outside with her red-ribboned braid and her pretty red skirts, holding a large bottle of milk. She started to speak, then stopped as she looked Liesel over.

"What is it?" Liesel snapped.

"I came to bring you this." Heike held out the milk. "You didn't look well yesterday."

"Of course I didn't. My brother is dead."

"I'm sorry, I know that, I just . . ." Heike peered past Liesel, into the little house with its rotting furniture and no light. Liesel shifted to block her view. Heike continued, "I thought something comforting might help. My mother always gave me milk when I felt poorly, so I thought I could warm some for you." Her fingers tapped against the bottle, and she glanced down into it as if she might find something there.

Liesel stared hard at her. She and Heike had played together as children, but they'd never been friends. She'd never liked how Heike always had the brightest skirts and that neat braid her mother did for her every morning. It was insufferable. Some of them didn't have mothers to warm milk for them and braid their hair.

"I don't want anything from you," Liesel said. "Go back to the forest."

Heike's expression turned sour. She thrust the bottle over the threshold and held it there, arm extended. "You aren't the only one here with no family. You aren't the only one who knows what it's like to lose someone. I know we haven't gotten along before, but I thought you wouldn't feel so alone if—"

"I'm fine."

Liesel shut the door so fast, Heike didn't have time to withdraw her hand. Glass shattered. A bit of milk trickled in under the door. Heike cursed, and Liesel listened to the sound of her nice shiny boots scuffing against the stones as she stomped off.

Later that morning a herd of elk stampeded out of the north forest, bypassed Ulrich's house, and stormed through the center of the village. Any conversation about redberry bushes, Death in the forest, or the sudden onset of the previous night's storm was snuffed out by the strangeness of the stampede. Gottfried climbed to the roof of the inn to pick the beasts off with his rifle, cackling like a madman.

Ulrich and several other villagers spent the day checking the north woods for signs of what could have made the herd act as it had, whether that be a predator or something else. The rest of the village stood around gossiping. On her way to see Hans early that afternoon, Liesel did her best to avoid the people lingering in the streets, but as she neared the butcher's shop, she caught the eye of Ada Bosch, who had none of her children with her and looked frayed.

"Liesel, Liesel dear, you haven't seen Oliver, have you? He's been out of the house all morning and I'm worried he got caught in the stampede."

Liesel had to take a moment to cycle through Ada's children until the image of the youngest one came to her.

"No, I'm sorry." Liesel lowered her head and shouldered her way past Ada. "You should ask Wenzel; he sees more than I do."

Hans was in a surprisingly good mood when she found him filling the divots left around the butcher's shop by the elk. She'd only ever seen three expressions on Hans: vacant curiosity, frustrated anger, and unbridled glee. The glee was fading back into curiosity as he watched the village square.

"Do you have time for me today?" Liesel asked. She'd planned other words, nicer words, but face-to-face with him she couldn't get them out.

"Oh. Yes." Hans sat back on his heels, throwing a hand over his eyes to block the weak sunlight. "My father's busy with the elk Gottfried took down, so we don't have to go to the barn. Wasn't that amazing? All those elk?"

"Shouldn't you be helping him? That must be a lot of meat."

"No—he's angry at me." Hans rolled his eyes. "He thinks I stole another one of his knives. The little ones that Godric makes for him. Told me to stay out here until I decide to give it back to him."

Something down the street caught his attention and the expression on his face was immediately eclipsed by frustrated anger. Wenzel and Heike had come out of the inn and were making their way across the square.

"I *should* take one of those knives and plant it in the inn. Do you think my father would think Wenzel stole it? Maybe I could convince him Wenzel was going to trade it for something nice when the merchants came to town . . ."

"I think he'd think you put it there to frame Wenzel. Now are we going, or have you decided to sit here all day talking about elks and sabotage?"

Hans grumbled something she didn't hear, stood, and took her hand. He pulled her around to the back entrance of the shop, where he and his father lived.

The rhythmic *thump thump* of the butcher's knife accompanied them the entire time they spent in Hans's bed. Between the thumping and Hans's mechanical indifference, Liesel felt like she spent two hours there, though the sun had hardly moved in the sky. When they finished, Hans looked her over and said, "You should put your hair in a braid."

She clamped her lips shut and left. Hans didn't chase after her. Halfway home, she started to cry again, and didn't stop until she buried herself beneath the covers of her bed.

The storm did not reappear that night, but Tomas did.

Liesel had dragged his bed in front of the door again in case the wind picked up, and she'd fallen into a light and restless sleep. A knock roused her from her uneasy nightmares. It was prim, three short raps, like Heike's had been that morning, except even Heike would know better than to go around knocking on doors in the middle of the night.

Tomas sat on the edge of his bed, watching her. His glow filled the room, though his body looked shrunken, as if his insides had shriveled up and were leaking out his eyes. He looked starved. He looked dead. Liesel's breath caught like she'd been dunked in cold water. She held tight to her screams and sat up.

"You needed to tell me something," she said. "What was it?"

Tomas disappeared from the edge of his bed and reappeared on the edge of hers. His hand was close enough to grab hers where it rested on top of the sheets, though he didn't. It took all her willpower not to move away from him.

"Do you remember what father said about the children of Greymist Fair when we were young? Remember?" Tomas looked up at her, eyes pleading. "He used to say there were no wolves in the forest because they were all here, causing trouble. He said we were little wolves. I used to believe him. I was never afraid of the forest because I was a wolf, and nothing hunts wolves."

Liesel remembered her father coming home from long hours on the Klein farm, yelling about wolves and mayhem because he couldn't get his two children under control. His temper had always cowed her, but it had excited Tomas.

"I was afraid of the forest that day. Something was watching me, waiting. I was chased. There were two wolves. The first one was on all fours, huge and dark, but it disappeared when the second wolf appeared." Tomas touched his chest with the fingertips of his left hand. They circled his heart, miming tearing, ripping his chest open. "The second one stood on its hind legs like a man but had a great big belly like a pig, and its claws flashed in the light.

"The second wolf clawed into me. I leaked out. The wolf tore my clothes and took my shoes off, and then carried me into the forest. Not far from the road, just far enough that no one would come looking. The wolf covered me with leaves and branches. It's cold here, it's so cold here."

He scooted closer. He cried, and his insides gushed down his cheeks.

"You wouldn't run away, Liesel, would you? You wouldn't run away if you saw the second wolf."

"No, I wouldn't run."

"Please stop crying," he said. "It's so cold here already."

Liesel blinked and he was gone.

The next morning she dressed, gathered some water and bread, and set off down the west road before the sun came up.

three

Liesel had never spent much time on the road. When she was younger, the children of Greymist Fair had dared one another to see how far they could go to the east or the west without turning back. Liesel had gone only once, and when she'd rounded the first bend and was out of sight of the village, the hairs on her neck prickled. When she turned back, the road was longer than it had been before, and she couldn't see the village through the trees. Only when Tomas started calling to her did the trees part and the lanterns lead her home.

This time there was no one to call her home, so she imagined Tomas standing on the road at the edge of the woods, waiting for her.

The walk to the Idle River Bridge took hours. When she passed over the river and looked up, a heavy blanket of gray clouds covered the sky, but it was still bright enough for Liesel to know that it had to be nearing noon. The woods around her were still, the silence broken every now and then by distant calls of winter birds.

She stood in the center of the bridge and looked toward the other side, where Heike had found Tomas's clothes. Liesel allowed herself a moment to imagine him there, to imagine him broken and bloody and splayed, and then she shut the image away and continued walking.

There were bloodstains on the stones. The lantern hanging there seemed like it should have been brighter or hotter than the others, but it wasn't. She turned in a circle and peered into the gloom between the trees. Underbrush clustered around the roots and up against the side of the road near the lantern, so thick and wild it was a wonder it hadn't yet grown over the stones.

She kneeled near the bloodstains. The children of Greymist Fair were not unaccustomed to blood or death, but it was not the same knowing this was Tomas's blood. She took a few deep breaths. There—on one stone, so faint it might go unnoticed, were signs of smearing. The marks headed toward the right side of the road, where several branches had broken off a bush. Liesel got to her feet and went to investigate.

She didn't want to find Tomas. She didn't want to see what his body looked like now. But she also couldn't leave him for the animals and the elements. He deserved to be buried beside their parents. She slipped between the trees, forgetting the forest, forgetting the wargs, forgetting herself. *Far enough that no one would come looking.*

She found the spot by smell. It was a shallow indent in the forest floor, crusted with congealed blood and surrounded by a strewn mess of branches and leaves. There was evidence of more dragging, but this was erratic with no attempt at camouflage. The animals had beaten her there. By now, there would not be enough of Tomas's body left to recover.

Liesel raised a hand to wipe her eyes and found she wasn't crying. Her emotions were still there inside her, but walled off. She was alone. What was she without her family? Even Hans didn't care about her, if he ever had.

A wink of light in the brush caught Liesel's eye. Half-hidden beneath the leaves and dirt was a small knife. The handle was made of oak, and the blade had been freshly sharpened. It appeared to have been hastily cleaned because blood still smeared it. In the metal, so small she almost didn't see it, was a small flourish—the *G* that Godric etched in all his metalwork.

The wolf had dropped his claw.

Liesel turned the knife over in her hands, thinking of a wolf that walked on its hind legs with a belly like a pig, thinking of

Hans rolling his eyes in front of the butcher shop, thinking of Jürgen helping her break the cold ground for Tomas's grave.

Jürgen had lost a knife made by Godric.

Liesel sat by the well in the town square, watching the other villagers go about their business, Jürgen's knife hidden in the folds of her skirts. Jürgen kept his knives in his shop; anyone could have stolen it.

A crowd was gathering outside the bakery. Ada Bosch was there, sobbing into her hands. Consoling her were other women, many of whom Ada did not normally speak to. It took Liesel a moment to see the connection; those other women had also lost children. Some very recently, others over the years.

Lost children were not uncommon in Greymist Fair. Even if they knew not to venture into the forest, they could not stop the forest from taking them. This was the way it had always been.

Liesel thought it was a little premature for Ada Bosch to believe her son had been taken, but maybe it was easier that way. The longer you held on to hope, the more painful it became.

The door to the butcher's shop burst open, and Jürgen stomped out like a great fuming boar. When he saw Ada and the other women, he seemed to withdraw a bit in the face of their grief. Then he cast his gaze around, like he was checking to see if anyone had noticed his outburst, before he lumbered back inside his shop.

Liesel turned the knife in her hand. *A great big belly like a pig.* Jürgen had the biggest belly in town, and the comparison to a pig couldn't be a coincidence—not because of his stomach, but because of his face. No one else in Greymist Fair fit that description. What if Jürgen had complained of his stolen knife to cover himself?

Why would Jürgen have been chasing her brother through the forest?

# four

Liesel did not wait for Tomas to appear in his shroud. When the moon was high, she tied her hair back, laced up her boots, and slipped out into the windy night.

The woods roared. Windows rattled in their frames, and the water bucket clattered and snapped against the well's stone walls. Liesel worried fleetingly about the roof of her cottage, which had been leaking and would very likely tear off in a gale like this. But the worry fell away as quickly as it had come; she didn't much care what became of her house.

She kept the knife concealed in her skirts, even though there was no one to see her. Anyone who lived near the center of town had barricaded themselves in for the night, and most lights were out.

The butcher's shop was dark, as was the attached residence. Hans slept like the dead, even during storms, but Liesel wasn't as sure about Jürgen. She paused in the shadows, trying to decide how to get in. Finally, she settled on the shop. But when she crept around to the door, she found it locked. Jürgen's knife was thin enough to slip between the door and its frame and lift the latch. The creak as the door opened was lost to the wind.

The shop was dark and reeked of salt and copper and sawdust. Jürgen's business was one of opportunity: when hunters brave enough to venture into the woods came back with a kill, they gave it to Jürgen to butcher in exchange for the best cut of the meat. The remainder went to the first customers to arrive for it. Everyone traded and bartered in Greymist Fair. Everyone wanted meat, so Jürgen never lacked anything. Eggs, milk, wool, clothing, repairs to his shop and his house, new knives. Liesel had once heard Dagny joking that Jürgen must have gotten his wife in a trade, because there was no other way anyone would have married him.

Once upon a time, Liesel had thought this was unfair. Just because Jürgen was blustery and prone to anger didn't mean he didn't have something good inside him.

Now she thought she had been too charitable.

Behind the shop counter was a door. Next to the door, Jürgen kept several small candles. Liesel set the knife down and lit one, then realized with a breathy curse she was going to have to keep the knife in her pocket so she could cup her free hand around the flame and dim the light. She pocketed the knife, paused to listen for any noises in the house, then continued through the door behind the counter.

The reek intensified. The room was long and lined with butcher's blocks stained nearly black, meat hooks hanging from the ceiling. The floor was dark. Jürgen's many knives hung from the walls and seemed to grow out of wooden blocks; there were so many knives that Liesel wouldn't have known one was missing if she didn't have it in her pocket right at that moment. She crept into the room and jumped as the candlelight fell on a gaunt face on the floor.

She clapped her hand over her mouth to hold in her scream. Not a face. A skull. Maybe a deer. It was clean, stripped completely of flesh. On the long shelf above her, a row of similar clean skulls leered up at her with empty eye sockets. Perhaps the deer skull had fallen off. Liesel stepped gingerly around it.

There was a door to the left and another to her right. The one on the left led to the house. She'd seen it from the other side, knew where it would be in relation to everything else. The door on the right, though, she didn't remember. She knew the first floor of the house ran right up against the back of the shop, but there was a jut of the wall where this door should be, pushing up against the fireplace. Like a cutout for a stairwell.

There was no handle on this door. Hanging from it was a

jumble of hooks and rope, thick and heavy, as if the door wasn't supposed to be a door at all but just part of the wall.

Then Liesel realized that it was *supposed* to look like the wall. The only reason she had recognized it as a door was because of the sharp shadows cast by the candlelight that showed her the door's seam and the scuff on the stone floor beneath it that marked where it swung open.

Jürgen had a hidden door.

With the candle in one hand, she wedged the knife into the seam, levering the door open. It was heavy, and she had to move slowly to keep the hooks hanging on it from clattering together. When it finally opened, she was treated to a puff of the cold, musty air of deep earth. The wind howled outside. The bubble of light from her candle only extended down a few wooden steps. No sound came from the blackness below.

It couldn't be a cellar. No one hid their cellar door, unless they were Gottfried and were paranoid someone was going to steal from them. It couldn't hurt to check, though, just to see what was there. It was safer than going into the house, anyway, where Jürgen himself would be much more likely to appear.

Testing the steps to make sure they didn't squeak—even with the wind outside, Liesel didn't want to risk Jürgen catching the small sound of an intruder—she started down into the darkness, candle in front of her. Very quickly the wooden stairs and narrow walls gave way to dirt. The passage descended under the house, then began to turn, spiraling downward. She couldn't fathom how long it had taken to dig it. And Jürgen must have dug it himself; anyone who had helped him would have long ago spread word to the town about tunnels under the butcher's shop. Unless it was dug long ago. No longer hiding the light, Liesel held the knife in front of her, palm sweaty. The sound of the wind faded behind her.

The deep earth was quiet. She came to a gate made of heavy wooden beams, secured with a lock. The gate was roughly made, nothing like Ulrich's work, but looked solid enough. Beyond the gate was darkness, but she could sense the nearness of walls, the lowness of the ceiling. There was a fetid stench, like unwashed bodies and human waste. Cold settled in Liesel's bones. This was not a cellar, and the gate was not there to protect food stores.

Metal clinked. Liesel clamped her jaw shut. She became very aware of something watching her, something she couldn't see. She froze.

She heard the breathing.

five

Liesel backed away from the door, stumbling, gasping, the candle flame fluttering with the sudden movement. A small voice inside the room cried out, "No!"

The voice was young. A child. Metal clanked; chains shifting. Out of the darkness scrambled a thin, pale figure. It was a young boy, his hair freshly cut, his face smeared with dirt. More chains rattled. Small hands appeared from the darkness to grab at the boy's arms and shirt, to try to drag him back. He fought with them, scratched them away.

"Oliver?" Liesel breathed.

Oliver, Ada Bosch's youngest, turned back to her. He looked like death in the candlelight, his eyes black and deep. "Have you come to let us out?" he asked.

Liesel swallowed the bile that rose in her throat and took a step closer to the gate. "Us?"

Eyes appeared in the gloom, glinting in the light. Liesel counted three others, besides Oliver. She could not see their faces, but if they were other missing children, they had been here for quite some time.

"He keeps the keys on the wall there, behind you," said Oliver, pointing.

Liesel found them. A keyring hung from a peg nailed high on the wall, a ways back from the door, much too far and high for any of the children to reach. The two keys were heavy, old; it would be hard for Jürgen to carry them around on his person without anyone getting curious.

"How did you get here?" Liesel asked as she grabbed the keys. "Jürgen did this?"

One of the other boys nodded. His name was Curt; he'd been missing for almost two months. "He doesn't talk to us. But sometimes he comes down and takes us upstairs. The ones he takes—we don't see them again."

The larger key fitted into the gate lock and turned with a rusty squeal. Liesel froze and listened, but all was silent above her. She slipped into the room. The four children shrank away from her candle, hiding their eyes; there was no sign of candle or lamp or lantern down here, and no way at all for them to see sunlight. They probably didn't even know what time of day it was, or that there was a storm raging outside.

The smaller key unlocked the collars. They were odd bits of

iron crudely shaped. Like the door, the work of an amateur making do with what he had on hand and what he could craft himself. Liesel's hair stuck to the back of her neck and her forehead as she pulled the chains free. The collars had apparently been pried open by brute force long enough to snap them around skinny necks, and she wasn't strong enough to open them again. The children tolerated her, though Oliver was the only one who regarded her with any kind of trust. The other three, hair and clothes ragged, eyed her like wild animals, unsure if they were being led to another trap.

When their chains were off, Liesel held out her hand. "Come," she said. "Hold hands. Stay together."

Oliver grabbed her hand without hesitation. The sensation made her shiver; it could have been Tomas instead of Oliver. The others were more wary, but eventually followed.

She led them back up the winding tunnel. She lost track of how far they had gone and nearly crashed into the closed door at the top. She paused, confused. She was sure she had left the door open. She *should* have closed it, because anyone who came through the cutting room would see it open and know someone had gone inside.

Could have been the wind, she thought.

That door is too heavy and the wind isn't getting into this room.

Carefully, she pressed her weight into the door and was

relieved to find it opened. She peered through the crack and saw and heard nothing beyond.

Maybe the door is so heavy it swings back into place.

She pushed the door open far enough to slip through. The room was empty. She urged the children out of the tunnel. Their eyes were huge. The howl of the wind outside sounded like demons descending on the village. Liesel shepherded them to the butcher's shop, glancing back at the house door as she did so. It was closed, too, as it had been.

The deer skull watched her from the shelf.

Screams erupted. She dashed after the children toward a hulking shadow holding Oliver aloft by the neck, little feet pounding against the shop counter. The others huddled behind the counter, screaming.

Liesel dropped her candle for her knife, threw herself at the round, heaving belly, and stabbed. The flesh parted easily. He dropped Oliver, bellowing in pain, and something heavy collided with Liesel's head. She blinked—the room was spinning—she was on the floor, breathing sawdust. The shadow loomed over her, the knife protruding from its stomach. A dark hand reached for her.

Three children launched themselves over the counter and tore into the shadow, hair and clothing, skin and bone. Liesel lunged forward and grabbed the handle of the knife, tore it out. The shadow man roared.

"*OUT!*" Liesel yelled. "*ALL OF YOU OUT NOW.*"

The children slipped from the shadow man like snakes, disappearing through the shop door slamming in the wind. Oliver picked himself up, but he wouldn't be fast enough to get out on his own.

The man charged. Liesel dove for the floor; the man crashed into the far wall. Liesel scrambled to Oliver, grabbed him, and hauled him outside.

He regained his feet quickly. Liesel shoved him away, hissing, "*Run home!*" He didn't think twice. Not a moment after he'd disappeared in the night did the shop door snap open again.

She ran for the center of town. She didn't know where else to go at this time of night, when everyone was asleep and the wind was so loud it could steal screams. Her head was still ringing. She stumbled every few steps, but she was faster than the gutted pig—for now.

The well appeared from nothing. Liesel hit it so hard her knees buckled. She caught herself from falling. She spun, dropped to the ground against its rough exterior, and held her arms braced, knife out.

She'd guessed right. He was behind her, and as she dropped,

she ducked below his stomach. He speared himself on her knife right at the juncture of his legs. There was a gasp, a sudden impact of weight against the stone well, and a shift of momentum. The knife was ripped from Liesel's hands. The shadow man tipped— shouted—disappeared.

There was scraping, several thuds, and finally a heavy splash. Then only the wailing of the wind.

Shaking, Liesel got to her feet. The well was deep enough that even the most fit among them would not have been able to climb out, not with the slick, cold stones that lined the inside. Her ears ached from the cold. She touched the side of her head and her fingers came away wet. She didn't feel well. She needed to vomit, and then sleep for a very, very long time. She turned and looked down into the well. There was only darkness. The wooden bucket banged against its post.

She thought she heard quick footsteps nearby. She looked up. Her vision swam.

"Tomas?" she called out.

Two hands settled on her back, firm and bony, never warm. She knew those hands.

Liesel tipped like an empty bottle over the lip of the well, into darkness.

six

In Greymist Fair there are many stories about wolves and children. In some the children *are* wolves, little terrors who must be taught how to eat, drink, and speak in civilized ways. Who must learn trades, maintain a home, and, eventually, raise little wolf children of their own to keep their history alive.

In other stories, older stories, the children *become* wolves. These are the children who are lost, who are murdered in their innocence. Their tormented souls cannot depart this world, for the claws of the forest hold them fast. In the old stories, they are the Wargs of Greymist, and they guide those who stray back to safety. In these stories, the wargs belonged to no witch. They were not evil.

It has been a long time since then. The wargs serve Death now.

The morning after the violent storm, the children from the butcher's basement are reunited with their families, and the details of their ordeal revealed. The butcher's house is searched, his vile cellar uncovered. The murder of the boy Tomas is revisited and attributed to the butcher's bloody hands. The butcher's body is pulled from the well, and steps are taken to determine how badly it contaminated the water. The butcher's son is questioned but knows nothing, and only looks at his father's pale corpse with vague curiosity. Some wonder if he has the intelligence to mourn. Others know he does and are repulsed by his lack of emotion.

The butcher's son wonders if his father's bones will look like bigger versions of the ones he has collected over the years. Bones from little fingers and toes, ribs, teeth. Bones his father tried to hide behind the house.

The freed children insist their savior fell into the well with the butcher. One says she was pushed by a third person of the same size and bearing as the butcher's son, but no one believes this. There are no other bodies in the well. There was an old dress caught on the butcher's body, but no one can be sure whose it is or where it came from. If there were shoes, they sank out of sight. A solution is offered: she climbed out. She went home.

But no one could have climbed out of that well, and she is not home. Her cottage is in shambles, the thatched roof torn off, one wall collapsed. Dirt and debris litter the interior. There is no sign of life here. No one has seen the young woman who saved the children from the butcher. No one will ever see her again.

Later in the week, over drinks at the inn, someone posits the theory that she died in the struggle with the butcher and then turned into a warg and ran off. That would explain the dress. Someone else disagrees; she was not a child anymore, and only children turn into wargs. Of course, the first person says. Right. You have to be a child. That's why the butcher wasn't taken, either.

But they are drunk and mistaken. The forest does not care about age. Children and adults alike have become wargs, but only if they are of Greymist Fair. Only if they claim the village, and the village claims them.

The butcher was left behind because the forest didn't want him. He had given up the right to call Greymist Fair home. But Liesel: she belonged.

Katrina

one

On a beautiful spring day, with wildflowers blooming in the fields and orioles heralding a rare and strong wash of warm sunlight on the village of Greymist Fair, Lady Greymist gave birth to a daughter who would be called the loveliest child in the world.

The first person to say so was the midwife, Gabi, who exclaimed with stunned surprise over Lady Greymist's gasps for breath, "I've never seen a fresh bloody babe so pretty."

The child was cleaned and given to her mother, who was enraptured with her upon first sight, as was the entire household staff. But perhaps the person most enamored with the girl was her father, the large and boisterous Lord Greymist, who spoiled her from that day forward.

They named her Katrina, after the lord's grandmother. She had her mother's olive complexion, her father's stunning dark eyes, raven's wing hair, and rosebud lips. Those who saw her even as an infant felt compelled to mention the grace of her proportions and the desire they felt to look upon her, to feel the softness of her skin and the silk strands of her hair. This effect only grew with her, so that even the servants who saw her every day remarked often on her great beauty. The lord and lady gave Katrina no siblings, for they felt they should not tempt fate when they had already been delivered perfection. They took her on walks around the village, and soon she became not just their daughter but the jewel of the Fair, lavished with praise and compliments and gifts. Even when Lord Greymist made an unpopular announcement about the smaller apportionments of the summer crop or the redirection of lumber to complete the extended wing of his manor, the villagers never took out their frustrations on Katrina. Having her along with him was a sure way to quell their anger.

Few people said anything about Katrina's personality. They were often too busy admiring her beauty to notice what she did or said, and she learned of this strange invisibility very early in her life. When she was small, she remained quiet, because no one listened to her when she spoke. But after thirteen, fourteen, fifteen years, she no longer had the patience to remain quiet.

"MOTHER," she yelled across the dinner table, where her mother sat idly sipping broth and smiling, unfocused, in Katrina's direction. Lady and Lord Greymist both jerked upright, her mother dropping her spoon and splattering the front of her gown.

"Katrina, you don't have to yell," her mother said, shakily

dabbing at herself as footmen stepped forward to clean the spill and retrieve the spoon from the floor. "I'm right across the table. We'll have to call Luther to make sure I'm not losing my hearing from this din you've been causing."

"Yes, you're sitting there, but do you remember what I've been *saying* to you?" Katrina looked between her parents.

Her father, puffing up his great round body and turning red behind his bristly mustache, said, "Of course we know, we wouldn't have been sitting here not listening—"

"So what did I say?"

"You said," her mother began, then stopped abruptly, shutting her mouth, as if that was all she had intended to say. Then her brow furrowed, and she said, "Was it about the kennel dogs?"

Katrina huffed. "I said I want to go out on my own. Without either of you."

The lord and lady glanced at each other. "Whatever for?" Lady Greymist asked. "Your studies are here; your books are here; all your gowns and instruments are here. I won't abide you running *errands*; we'd look like we're punishing you."

That might well turn the villagers against them, Katrina thought, annoyed. "I just want to be on my own for a while. I want to—" She huffed again, hating that she didn't sound more mature. "I want to make friends. There are plenty of others in the village who are my age. I want to talk to *them*."

Lord Greymist shifted in his chair, puffed up like an angry bird. "And who would this be that you've got your eye trained on, then?"

"Does it matter?"

"It certainly *does* matter," snapped Lady Greymist, her anger not directed at Katrina but at the villagers she chose to detest behind closed doors. "God forbid you be seen with the witch-slave's daughter or with that innkeep servant boy."

Katrina pursed her lips. Heike and Wenzel had, in fact, been at the top of her list, the two of them being the most interesting young people in town, by her estimation.

"I *will* go out," she said. "At least once a week. And I'll see who I want."

Apparently forgetting to argue—her parents and tutors often did that, starting an argument with her only to forget halfway through what they were arguing about, or even that they were arguing—Lady Greymist looked pensively into her broth and said, "Someone of good breeding, from the houses, no one from the outskirts of the village."

Her father, nodding, said, "Of course, of course."

"What about Hans?" said her mother, looking up, eyes bright. "Jürgen is a great asset to this community, with a good livelihood and a strong build. Hans is quiet like his father, though I must say thankfully he gets his looks from his mother's side."

"Hans would be a good match, I think," said her father.

Katrina ground her teeth together. She didn't want to *marry* anyone; she only wanted to talk to them, on her own terms, without her parents hovering over her shoulder, carefully maneuvering her around like a pretty porcelain doll that might crack at the slightest jostle. And she especially didn't want to marry *Hans*, who was handsome but dull eyed and cruel. Still, she knew her parents had softened; now she could get what she wanted out of them.

"I'll talk to Hans," she said, and added nothing at all about also planning to talk to every other young person she saw. "And I will go out into the village *on my own*."

Her parents, finally, begrudgingly, agreed.

two

On a brisk spring day, when the village bustled with its morning routines and the orioles trilled in the leaves, Katrina set out from Greymist Manor with her hair gathered up in sky-blue ribbons, her favorite dress swishing against her ankles, and the faintest blush of rouge lighting her cheeks. She carried a wicker basket in the crook of one arm, thinking she might stop by the Kleins' stall in the square for a few fresh apples, or the bakery for a pie, which she could bring home as proof to her parents that she was well capable of navigating the village on her own.

Gottfried, the hunter, was the first person to see her, and he stopped in his tracks. The Great Dane puppy that followed him—one from a manor litter that Lord Greymist had traded for a great rack of antlers now positioned over the fireplace—crashed into his legs and flopped onto its haunches, stunned.

"Lady Katrina," Gottfried said, bending swiftly at the waist, a perfect ninety-degree angle of deference. His hat slid down his gray-streaked hair, and he caught it just before it hit the ground.

"I should have known you would be out; the orioles were saying so all morning, but I didn't listen to them."

He was a strange man, Gottfried, and had been for as long as Katrina could remember. But anyone who braved the woods as often as he did had to be at least slightly insane.

She gave him a graceful short bow back, smiling, and said, "How is Oswald? I heard his berry patch is already showing promise."

Gottfried beamed at mention of his husband. "Aye, it is, and I'll tell him to bring some to the manor when they're ripe! He'll be joyed to hear you asked after him, Lady Katrina."

They shared a few more kind remarks and then Katrina went on her way, Gottfried loping off in the other direction with the puppy—he had named it The Duke, quite a big name for a puppy, Katrina thought—and whistling a merry tune not unlike the orioles' song.

As Katrina crossed the square, she felt eyes turning to her, attentions drawing away from whatever they had been doing to watch her pass. She was very used to this phenomenon, as it happened whenever she went out with her parents. She had hoped, at times, that everyone would get used to the way she looked, that she could at some point be both beautiful *and* normal, thought pretty and not fussed over, but she wondered if she would miss the attention. If something would feel wrong were everyone *not* to notice when she entered a room, or when she turned her soft gray gaze on them.

Now was her chance, though. To be beautiful *and* to be seen. Her conversation with Gottfried had gone well enough; someone her own age would see her for exactly who she was.

There weren't many people her age in the village, though. There was Hans, of course, the butcher's son, who Katrina had always found annoying and—she knew the irony was strong— spoiled. There was a girl, Liesel, who lived somewhere south of the bakery, but she always looked hassled, dragging her little brother, Tomas, on errands around the village. Then there was the fisherman's son, Fritz, but he was spineless and soft and spent too much time with Hans, besides. It amazed Katrina how much she had picked up about her neighbors from the walks with her parents and the news they mulled over each night at dinner and each morning at breakfast. She felt as if, by observing the village around her, she had always been part of its inner happenings, had always known how it worked and why.

The two people she was looking for were out and together. Heike sat on the stone wall in front of the inn, and Wenzel stood in front of her, leaning on his broomstick and gesturing with his hands, probably reciting one of the many stories he'd picked up from the traveling merchants. There was such ease in their near-ness, in the way Wenzel stood between Heike's swinging legs, but not so close as to be indecent or suggestive; in the way Heike leaned forward and tilted her head back to see him, squinting one eye against the glare of the sun.

They were, Katrina had always felt, the antithesis of her. Not that they weren't beautiful—she didn't really think anyone was ugly or deserved to be called such, and Wenzel and Heike would only have been called ugly by someone who wanted to hurt them—but because they could blend into their surroundings where she could not. They always seemed to have so many *real* things to do, real responsibilities that callused their hands and put dirt on their faces; and, most of all, they had someone who understood them. They had each other. They had easy touches and routines and a silent language that could make them burst out laughing in the middle of the midsummer feast on the village green. She wanted what they had so badly, it was a physical ache in her chest.

She put on a smile and made her way toward them. Heike noticed her first, those gold hawk eyes focusing on Katrina. Wenzel turned. His expression was first blank, then surprised, then welcoming. He smiled.

"Katrina!" he called, which sent frothy bubbles of excitement spinning around her stomach, making her skip across the square. When she reached them, Wenzel looked troubled. "Or—should I call you Lady Katrina?" He turned to Heike then, as if she could give him the answer.

"My parents would make you add the 'lady,'" Katrina said, winking conspiratorially at him, "but I'm okay if you don't." How would she ever make friends if they were always reminded of her title?

"Is everything okay?" Heike asked, cocking her head the same way Katrina had seen her mother, Hilda, do from time to time. "Are your parents okay?"

She sounded genuinely concerned, which made Katrina's excitement grow. "No, they're perfectly fine! I convinced them to let me come out on my own today." The excitement stuttered and so did she; they were looking at her, waiting for her to continue, but she sounded suddenly childish to her own ears. "I suppose that seems . . . silly. They think I'm some kind of doll to be kept on a shelf. . . ." Now she was blurting her problems to them, problems that probably—no, that *were*—very minimal to two people who had to work every day for their clothes and food and shelter. "I'm sorry, this was a poor way to start a conversation. I'm afraid I'm not very good at it."

Wenzel waved his hands, one still holding his broom. "No,

no! It's fine, it's just"—he looked at Heike again, who gave him that level, gold gaze—"we've never really gotten to speak to you before."

Katrina blinked, for a moment feeling very airy and stupid, though she knew she wasn't, and during that moment her perspective of her memories shifted very slightly. She was so used to seeing the other villagers, watching them, observing them from afar and spending so much of her time putting together the pieces of their lives in her mind, that she had forgotten they didn't know her. Maybe they didn't even wonder about her life the way she did about theirs; maybe all they saw of her really was her beauty.

"Oh," she said, her excitement gone flat.

"It's nice to talk to you now, though," said Heike quickly, to which Wenzel nodded. "Before you came up, I was showing Wenzel my new boots." She thrust a leg up in the air. Her foot was inside a sturdy leather boot, laced up tightly at the top, with a bit of green ribbon woven through the eyelets. "Well, they're not *new* new; they were my mother's. My old ones weren't even bursting at the soles, and she gave these to me." A little knot of confusion formed between Heike's eyebrows.

"Two good pairs of shoes!" Wenzel yelped comically, throwing his arms up. "And you're complaining?"

Heike smiled and used the extended boot to push his hip, putting him off-balance. Katrina smiled, too, but felt as if she was standing outside the joke, as if the two of them had drawn back into their own world. She wondered what their wedding day would be like, because she was certain they were going to get married. It would be on the green behind the inn, of course, as all the weddings were. Heike would wear a crown of wildflowers, purples and yellows and reds, and Wenzel would get two bear claws or bits of elk antler or rabbit's feet. The bear claws were the luckiest, but the elk antler wasn't bad and a much more likely find, while the rabbit's feet were for those who may as well have been forced into marriage. They'd get them from Gottfried or someone else, and Wenzel would present them on leather cords that he and Heike would wear around their necks until they died or separated, a symbol that they were of the forest, and of each other.

Katrina stopped herself. She was fantasizing, again, about these people she thought she knew, instead of talking to them like she had come to do.

"They're very nice," she told Heike. "The boots."

Heike shrugged and hopped off the stone wall. She was taller than Katrina, and solidly built; Katrina had to stop herself from imagining Heike going about her daily chores, strong enough to lift anything she came across. "I better get back," Heike said. "I'll get yelled at if she thinks I'm fooling around in the middle of the day again."

Hilda yelled at her daughter? Katrina had never seen that. She filed the information away.

"Wait," Katrina said, before Heike and Wenzel could go back to their work. "I was wondering, since I'm going to be out more, if you'd like to—well, I thought maybe we could spend some time together? We could go down to the lake, or we could take a stroll around the village, or tell each other stories. . . ."

She let her voice trail off, because they were staring at her again, that vague blank stare that told her she'd made some kind of misstep.

"I can't today," Heike said, looking sheepish. "I actually shouldn't have spent as much time here as I did."

"Neither can I," Wenzel said, shrugging. "We're doing repairs on the roof. It's been leaking for weeks."

Katrina hadn't really meant *today*, but their answers seemed to convey the proper sentiment anyway. She wasn't one of them; they made time for each other and didn't have enough left over for her. How could she blame them? If she was the one who had what she needed, why would she pollute it with more?

But she had thought they would, for her. She had always, eventually, gotten what she wanted. As long as someone looked at her long enough, as long as she could hypnotize them.

But no matter how long Wenzel and Heike looked, she knew her beauty didn't faze them.

She put on a happy smile and said, "That's too bad. Maybe another time," and left them to their many responsibilities. She tried not to feel too sore about it, but she *was* sore; rejection had hurt more than she had imagined it would.

Instead of a pie, she went to the bakery and bought one of Johanna's apple pastries and sat in the square nibbling on one crimped corner. Her mother always said she was beautiful no matter what mood she was in, and she—her mother, not Katrina—was proud of that fact. Katrina supposed the people looking at her now were doing so because she was a pretty girl eating prettily, not because she looked upset. Even if she threw the pastry and screamed and tore at her hair, they would just say how beautiful she was, how graceful. Her parents had already done so. Tantrums got her nothing.

So she was sitting, scowling—though it probably didn't look like it—toward the well in the center of the village, when she felt a presence come near.

"Hi, Katrina."

She looked up. Hans smiled at her.

"Do you want to see something interesting?" he asked.

three

On a chilly spring day, with the wind whipping whitecaps across Grey Lake and the orioles shuttering themselves in the trees, Katrina became friends with Hans, the butcher's son. He had always made her uncomfortable, and there was something strange about his eyes, but he was available, and he promised her something she wouldn't forget. Perhaps *friends* was too strong a word for what they were, but Katrina had never had friends, so this was as close as she had ever been.

They walked south to the lake together, where they met Fritz, the fisherman's son, untangling nets by the dock. While Hans was of perfectly average height and proportions, blond hair neatly cut and parted, his face and clothes clean of dirt, poor Fritz looked as if he'd been grabbed by the head and feet and stretched until his bones no longer connected. A streak of grime ran over his cheek and up his long nose. Dark strings of hair hung into his dark, frightened eyes, which were like the eyes of a rabbit.

Fritz saw them coming and immediately froze, rabbit eyes

darting toward a shack nestled up against the trees.

"You shouldn't be here now!" he hissed. "My father will—"

"Your father is puking fishes," Hans said, full volume, gesturing back toward the shack. "I'll bet Doctor Death is still in there, isn't he?"

Fritz's tight-lipped silence confirmed this. Fritz dropped the nets and, as if he already knew why Hans was here, motioned them down the northern lakeshore. As he strode off the dock, he cast poorly concealed glances toward Katrina, as if he couldn't believe she was there.

The shore was gray and rocky, strewn with dead branches. Katrina's basket bounced against her leg as she followed Fritz. Soon after they set off, the uneven beach disappeared entirely, replaced by a steep wall of tree roots and earth, the forest pressing over the edge of the lake. Katrina saw—and smelled—what waited for them at the far end of the lake before they reached it: a carcass of some dead creature, bigger than Katrina herself, mostly picked away so the skeleton leered out between ribbons of rotted flesh. She held her hand under her nose, trying to ward off the thick musk of death with the butter and yeast scent of the apple pastry, and watched Hans hurry almost giddily forward. Why this? Why had he thought she would be interested in seeing this?

But when they reached the creature, she understood. She had thought perhaps that it was a bear that died and fell, somehow, into the lake, only to resurface. But up close, it was no bear; it had flippers, for one thing, three on either side of a long, round body. A great slab of flesh had been carved from its flank, showing its ribs, and much of the other skin had been picked off by scavengers. It had a long neck, curled up and around itself, the vertebrae now only held together by strings of graying meat. A round head and a short snout filled with razor-sharp teeth. And it must have also had a tail, a long one, but those vertebrae disappeared into the water.

She had never seen anything like it. She looked out over the lake with a shiver. Had it been here the whole time? What else dwelt beneath the water?

"What is it?" Katrina asked, looking at Fritz.

Fritz jumped when he realized she had addressed him. Rubbing his hands together, he said, "I'm n-not sure, Lady Katrina. I've never seen anything like it. Neither has my father. He thought it would be good meat, but he got sick when he tried to eat some. That's why Doctor Luther is with him now."

"It showed up—what, two days ago?" Hans said, looking to Fritz for confirmation, though he didn't wait for an answer. "We think it must be a sign of the witch."

Fritz blushed at this.

Katrina looked between them, the stench forgotten. "Really? You really think this is—this creature was created by magic?" Now that *was* interesting, and she felt bad for doubting Hans.

"Fritz says he has *never* seen anything like this on the lake before, and neither has his father. And his father is as ancient as the town! When strange things happen, the witch is to blame!"

"Then why hasn't Falk told anyone else about it yet?" she asked.

Fritz made a strangled noise. Hans continued to talk over him. "You start telling everyone there's witchcraft in the lake and no one will want to eat fish anymore. And maybe that's a good thing, if even his putrid father—Falk—got sick from it. Maybe the witch is trying to poison the food supply." Hans's eyes lit up, and for the first time he looked truly *alive*, truly part of the world he stood in. "This appeared now because she's casting her spells again. Maybe the tailor hasn't been doing a very good job."

Fritz started. "She is still going, isn't she? Hilda? Into the woods to talk to the witch?"

Hans sneered at him. "You shake any harder, Fritz, you're going to shake your own skin right off. Calm down; she still goes into the forest."

"Nobody has ever . . ." Katrina paused, wondering if she was about to sound very naive. "Nobody has ever seen the witch, besides Hilda, have they?"

Fritz shrugged. Hans said, "No, not unless they're in league with the witch and hiding it." This made Fritz rake both hands through his hair.

"Do you think there really is a witch?" Katrina asked.

They both stared at her, and then Hans burst out laughing, which made Fritz smile nervously. "Of course there's a witch!" Hans said. He motioned to the creature's corpse. "How else do you explain this? Or the frosts in the middle of summer that kill the crops? Or the ravens that follow you around, gathering all your secrets?"

Katrina had never known the weather to be particularly stable in Greymist Fair, and she didn't think there was a way to prove the ravens were gathering secrets, but she didn't have any explanation for the dead creature.

Hans was pacing around the creature now, his arms crossed. Katrina wanted to tell him to stop; it seemed the creature might come alive at any moment and bite off his leg. "Can you imagine what it must be like, to have the power to create living things? To change the weather, or make animals your familiars? Do you think the witch was born with magic, or did she learn it?" Hans asked.

Katrina and Fritz glanced at each other. Fritz shrugged.

"What would you do with magic, if you had it?" Hans asked them. He'd stopped, feet planted, near the creature's head.

"I—I dunno," Fritz said.

"Of course you do," Hans snapped. "Everyone knows what they would do if they could do anything. What would it be?"

Fritz, shuffling in place and looking around as if an answer might be somewhere near him, at last said, "I guess I'd make myself stronger. Then I could build a better boat."

Hans rolled his eyes. "What about you, Katrina?"

"I would make myself like everyone else," she said, without hesitation.

Hans's eyebrows furrowed. "What for? It's better to be special."

"Well, what would *you* do with magic?" Katrina shot back, motioning with her basket. "Your father has provided you with a house to live in, you have fine clothes, plenty to eat. What would *you* want that isn't silly or simple?"

Hans's lips parted to reveal his crooked teeth. He spread his arms wide. "I would make myself the King of Greymist! I would hold feasts every night, and the whole village would dance and sing. I could invite anyone I wanted to my table, I could appoint whomever I wanted as my servants, I could *have* anyone I wanted. Even my father wouldn't be able to tell me what to do, the cruel bastard."

He looked so young, and he sounded so serious, that Katrina started laughing. Hans dropped his arms and flushed red from his collar to his hairline. He glared at Fritz, who had to turn his laughs into coughs.

"You think the witch would teach you how to use magic so you could go and make yourself king?" Katrina wiped her eyes, barely breathing through the last of her laughter. "Well, actually, maybe she would. That would be a fast way for her to burn Greymist Fair to the ground."

"You think she'd teach *you* just so you could make yourself like everyone else?" Hans said. "She'd turn you into a toad for such a stupid request."

Katrina folded her hands on the handle of her basket. "Would you like to bet on that? I think she'd laugh in your face."

"I'd happily wager my life on that." Hans's chest was puffed up, his chin thrust out, pride and defiance in his eyes. "You and I, Katrina, we'll go to the witch's home in the forest. I'll find the way. We'll ask her to make us students, then let her decide who she'll take. And we're betting our lives on it."

Of course we will, Katrina thought, pursing her lips to

keep from smiling again. She was absolutely sure that Hans would never find the path to the witch's home, and they would never go to her, and there would never be a winner or a loser. Hans was marching his ego around, and this grand declaration was all that would ever come of it.

Two weeks later, she was proven wrong.

four

On a dark spring day, with the clouds scudding across an overcast sky and the orioles complaining from their hiding spots, Katrina crept after Hans past the hill upon which sat Hilda's cottage. It looked gray and ramshackle, tiny compared to Greymist Manor, and Katrina felt like Hilda was watching them from its windows and knew what they were doing.

"I know the way. I know how to get to the witch," Hans had said when he'd found her taking her walk through the square the week before. "I don't know what everyone is so scared of. It's just some *trees*. Only the weak fear the forest."

He had followed Hilda when she went on her visit. He had remained close enough so as not to get lost, close enough to call out to her if he got into danger, but the forest hadn't seemed dangerous at all.

They had come to a cottage deep in the woods, in a clearing where all the trees were losing their leaves, as if it was fall. The cottage was nothing to look at, he said. Like any other cottage in the village.

"She didn't go inside. She tied some plants to a string on the door and then walked around the outside a few times. It didn't take very long at all. It's no wonder the witch is putting monsters in the lake—the tailor isn't even talking to her anymore!"

Katrina's stomach flipped as she and Hans crept closer and closer to the forest's edge. She had never been this close to the trees before; they seemed to touch the sky, their highest branches bending to a wind she couldn't feel here on the ground, their leaves rustling from an invisible touch. Since she had offered the bet, she had considered what she would do if she won it—what *would* she do with magic, besides making herself normal? And what did that even mean, *normal*? She still wanted to be beautiful, but she also wanted to have friends, and to be allowed to go out whenever she chose, and she wanted people to listen to her when she spoke—but she hadn't thought that Hans would figure out how to get to the witch. Katrina had not considered the actual journey.

Fritz had refused to go, despite Hans's nearly constant harassing. "I don't go in the forest. Da says no forest, so I don't go in the forest. There's enough weird things coming out of the lake; I don't want to see what's in the forest. People get killed in there, you know?"

Katrina knew—even if she didn't know about the witch, she knew the forest itself was not worth the risk for most of the villagers—and Hans should have known, but either he had chosen to ignore the warnings, or he believed they didn't apply to him.

And now here they stood, at the first of the trees, with the village at their backs. Hans dove in without hesitation. Katrina scanned the hazy blue shadows between the trunks, listened for sounds deep from those unknown places of tunneling roots and twisting branches. There was no movement, and the sound was a low-volume hum of insects and wind broken only by the low hoot of an owl that Katrina could have imagined.

The walk was long, and the chill settled under Katrina's clothes not long after Greymist Fair disappeared behind them. Once inside of it, she didn't find the forest as scary as she'd expected. There were birdcalls, and the soft rustle of leaves, sounds not so different from the ones she heard out her window every morning. Hans never went too far from her, always turning to make sure she was still there, holding out a hand to help her over fallen trees and down sudden slopes.

To mark their path, Hans had brought small white sticks wrapped with red string that he tied to bushes and low branches.

When the last marker had almost been swallowed by the forest behind them, he hung another. The bag slung across his chest was full of them. Katrina paused to looked closer at one after he hung it. The little stick was knobbly at one end and jagged at the other and hollow on the inside. She couldn't think of what tree or bush it had come from, but then she realized it wasn't a stick: it was bone.

"My father gives me a lot of the bones from the animals he butchers," Hans said when she asked. "I put them in the sun so they turn white, and then I make things out of them. You should come see them sometime—they're good."

"Are you sure this is the way?" Katrina asked when his bag hung limp and nearly empty and the trees curved together over-head. "We've been walking for a long time. You said before that Hilda only stayed for a few hours—"

"There!"

Hans darted forward. Heart in her throat, Katrina hurried after him. Past the fall of low branches and light-starved undergrowth, the forest opened suddenly into a perfectly round clearing. Katrina stumbled, gasping; she could have sworn moments ago that the trees continued on, that this clearing could not exist. But they were standing here now, the sky like a steely pot lid clasped down over the rim of the treetops, and in the middle of the clearing was a cottage.

It was just like the cottages in the village, as Hans had said, but it wasn't *only* like the cottages of the village: it was one cottage specifically. Hilda's. There was no mistaking it. The old stones in its walls, the way the thatched roof was beginning to come apart on one side, the herbs tied to the door, and the tree—the exact same linden tree as stood atop the hill, with the same twist to its trunk, the same three low branches reaching out to shade the area beneath it. Had Hans not noticed when he'd come last time? Why would the cottage look exactly like Hilda's?

Hans had paused on the edge of the clearing, Katrina only a few steps behind him.

"She'll already know we're here," he said. "No point in hiding. I suppose it'd be best to knock on the door, don't you? Katrina?"

He turned, frowning at her. She was frozen to her spot. The birds had stopped singing. The wind had died. The hum of the forest was gone. It was as if, by crossing the threshold from the trees to the clearing, they had entered another world. They were not supposed to be here. The cottage itself was too quiet; without the wind or the birds, she could hear Hans breathing, felt like she could hear the clouds moving across the sky. There was no light in the small windows, no scuffing of feet or clank and rattle of instruments. Perhaps the witch was sleeping, but in the middle of the day? This was wrong. Something was wrong here.

Hans grabbed her hand, jolting her out of her thoughts. "Come on. We're going." He dragged her across the clearing. Weeds caught on her skirts. She fought to remember why she was here, what had convinced her to come in the first place. Was this magic? Silence and foreboding? Even in the worst stories of the witch, there were incantations and thunder, the blood from beheaded magpies and the tails of rats, an immediacy to the action. The magic was always happening *now*. It was never like this, waiting, hunkered, like an animal with its eyes flashing in the gloom.

"No, Hans," Katrina said, yanking on his hand. He continued toward the cottage with an almost zealous pace. "Hans! This isn't safe—we need to leave!"

He couldn't feel it, she realized. He couldn't feel the chill of death.

Hans reached for the door.

"*STOP.*"

The voice came from behind them. The link between their hands burned white hot, so fierce and sudden they both gasped and whipped away from each other. Rushing from the veil between the trees was Hilda, her golden hair flying loose, her eyes wide and grim lines drawn across her face. "Stop!" she yelled again, but there was no flash of fire with it. "Don't go inside! You'll be killed!"

Hans shrank, cowed, but only for a second; a moment later he was inflating his chest and sticking his chin out. "And who are you to say what we can and can't do? Why are you the only one who can speak to the witch? Clearly, she knows we're here—if she wanted us dead, we'd be dead by now."

"Foolish boy!" Hilda reached them and grabbed Hans by the collar, dragging him back from the door despite his being taller than she was. Katrina moved away gladly but kept her distance from Hilda. "What did he promise you, Katrina?" Hilda asked. "Did he tell you this would be a fun adventure? Did he make it seem like he knew what he was doing? He doesn't. He's a stupid boy trying to impress you. You shouldn't have come here." She threw Hans away from the cottage, hard enough that he stumbled and fell into the grass and had to scramble to his feet. "Stupid, *stupid* boy!"

"I don't have to listen to you!" Hans snapped.

"Just as I expect from Jürgen's son," Hilda replied, marching on him, driving him back toward the trees. "You're as stubborn and cruel as your father. Go on, go home! Your little bone markers are gone, but you won't have any trouble, will you? You, who are too ignorant to fear death, you have nothing to worry about. You'll think of your warm bed and your fine house and you'll find your way without problem. Go! *Go!*" She flung her hand out, and Hans, ten feet away and backpedaling, toppled over as if she had shoved him. He pushed himself to his feet again, flushed with anger—had he not noticed that she was too far away to shove him?—and fled into the trees.

He deserted her so quickly. He hadn't even looked at Katrina before he'd gone. She was alone in the clearing now with Hilda and the cottage that was silent as death, and as Hilda turned to look at her, Katrina took another step sideways, toward the forest.

"Katrina," Hilda said, carefully.

"Your cottage looks like this one," Katrina said. She could not stay in this clearing any longer. Death was a hand on the back of her neck, stroking. "You—you made us burn. You pushed Hans down."

Hilda held out her hands as if to show they were empty. "Katrina, please. You're feeling something now, aren't you? You feel the cold? I know it can be frightening, but please, you mustn't go into the forest feeling this way. It won't be safe for you—"

But it wasn't safe *here*, either; Katrina knew that for sure.

There was no witch in the cottage. The witch was standing before her.

She hesitated for only one more moment.

Then she turned and bolted, and when she broke the threshold of the trees, death came for her.

five

On a dead spring day, the wargs began to laugh.

It was not normal animals that made the people of Greymist Fair so wary of the forest. Normal animals could be killed with weapons of wood and iron. Normal animals did not manifest from the deep bruises of the trees. Normal animals were not creatures of magic.

The beasts chasing her were wargs, Katrina knew, not wolves. She could see them running through the trees alongside her. They were cut from shadow, flat, darting from one trunk to the next. Black tongues lolled from smiling black snouts, and their eyes were blue flames. They laughed human laughs. The laughs of children and adults both; soft snickers, belly chortles, and, when Katrina stumbled, giddy shrieks.

Hilda's voice echoed through the branches, an incantation that dropped leaves from the trees and made Katrina's legs go numb. She could no longer remember why she had come here, or where she was trying to go. She no longer had ethereal beauty she hadn't asked for, no longer had coveted grace of movement. She was no longer friendless. She no longer had parents, a home, or a name.

She had fear. She had a body and a pulse inside that body that told her she must run. There was only survival or death.

The wargs laughed. They were in front of her, behind her, around her. Spirits of those the forest had claimed. They surrounded her, a ring of gaping teeth and corpse-fire eyes. She tripped, screamed, scraped herself up from the ground and kept going. The ring tightened. Her legs were so tired. Her knees burned. Tears blurred her vision. Where was she going? Where *could* she go? She remembered safety and warmth, but they seemed so far away now. She was no longer running but stumbling from tree to tree, hands bloodied, hair hanging in tangles around her face. She screamed for help and listened to her own voice echo endlessly, only to return as laughter.

At last, when her legs could no longer hold her, she skidded to her knees on the forest floor. Her fingers splayed in the hard-packed earth. Her nails were torn, her knuckles caked red. She knew she would not get up again, so she did the only thing left to her, and curled into herself, crying, allowing herself to be the small and weak thing she was.

This is all a dream, she thought wildly, in the last shred of her rational mind. *If I surrender to it, I will wake up. I only have to give in, and everything will be okay.*

She shut her eyes tight and put her arms over her head. Her ears rang with the laughter of the lost.

six

Hilda almost tripped over the body. The beautiful face was gone. The dress was torn, strewn about in the foliage. The ribcage spread like spiked petals of a gruesome flower. They liked doing that, the wargs—they liked prying the ribcage open. They didn't eat any part of the body, because they didn't need to. It was the fear they fed on.

There would be a new warg soon, and the only evidence that Katrina had been in the woods would be the scraps of her dress and her shoes.

Hilda backed up. Scanned the woods. The wargs had ignored her when there was ripe prey on the run, but they were coming back now, scenting her fear on the air. Because she did have fear. Even when she knew how to get home, she couldn't make it if she couldn't run fast enough. She didn't regret giving Heike her boots. She only wished she had waited a little longer, so she could tell Heike the other things she would need to know.

Her fear wasn't all-consuming. She had known Death would

catch her eventually. In the parts of her fear could not reach, there lived a deep, final annoyance:

This was how she went? After all this time, after everything, because a stupid boy had almost unwittingly unleashed Death on himself and Katrina? And poor Katrina had died anyway. There was no way to get a message back to town. Not to Heike, but to Luther. He was visiting Falk the fisherman and making his rounds of the village. She wished she could tell him what happened, tell him how little Heike knew. He wouldn't be able to teach her much, but he could do something. He could tell her the truth.

Well, she thought grimly, *I can't let myself die without having even tried to get home.* So she squared a thought of Heike in her mind and started running.

The laughter began again.

THE SECRET
OF GREY LAKE

one

"I want to be king of Greymist Fair. I want to live in the manor, except I want the manor to be a castle. I want Dagny and Johanna as my cooks. I want a feast every night. I want a dancing bear dressed in purple and gold as entertainment for my court. I want all the villagers to serve me in some fashion. I want—hm—I want that dirty innkeep as my whipping boy. And I want Heike as my personal tailor. Did you get all that? I told you to write it down!"

Fritz had written down most of it, but his hair had been in his eyes, making his strokes uneven and wobbly and, besides that, he couldn't write or read all that well in the first place. If he didn't keep looking at the oil-stained parchment he'd scribbled on, he would soon forget what he'd put there. The words looked silly. A king? Hans was really going to make good on that old wish? It had been ridiculous when they were fifteen, and it was even more ridiculous now.

"I c-can't ask for this," Fritz said. "Greymist Fair d-doesn't *have* a king."

"Are you refusing to do it?"

"I just . . . it seems like a bad idea. The other things were strange enough, but this changes everything. A-a-and a w-whipping boy? You can't keep the villagers as slaves."

"I suppose I also can't tell the village that you saw my father follow Tomas down the west road, and you did nothing to stop him," Hans said. Fritz's heart flopped in his chest. "They'd have some questions about that, wouldn't they? I suppose I also couldn't tell them that you went with my father. That you helped him catch Tomas."

"That's a l-lie!"

"They won't know that," Hans said.

Fritz *had* seen Jürgen follow Tomas down the west road that day, but he hadn't thought anything of it. And he certainly hadn't *helped* Jürgen with his vile schemes. Fritz had been coming home from the village square with an empty fish cart and had squatted discreetly behind a bush to relieve himself when he saw first Tomas trot by, then Jürgen wrapped in a cloak. They'd been far enough apart that it seemed like coincidence. Only later had he realized what he'd seen.

"Th-they won't believe you," Fritz warbled.

"Do you want to take that chance?" Hans stared at him.

No, he didn't. What would the town do to him if they

thought he'd helped Jürgen kill Tomas, or cage all those other children? What would his father do? What would Heike or Wenzel think of him? Now that both Katrina and Liesel were gone, Heike, Wenzel, and Hans were the only three his age left. They were all supposed to grow old together.

"Are you sure this is what you want?" Fritz asked, pleading now. "Y-you could get your parents back. Or you could just be rich. Or—"

"If I wanted you to decide my wishes for me, I would've said so." Hans bared his teeth, his eyes flashing. "Just *do it*."

They stood outside the fisherman's hut at the edge of the forest. Falk had gone into the village, stumping off on his wooden leg, and as soon as he left, Hans had appeared. Fritz knew why he was there—Hans only came to visit for one thing anymore—but that only made Fritz more reluctant to go out and talk to him. He had finished binding his chest, pulled on his shirt, and slumped outside with a crumpled paper and some charcoal.

"It'll take me some time," Fritz said. "It's getting h-harder to find."

Hans's lip curled. "Why don't you tell me where it is, and I'll fish it out of the lake myself?"

"It won't work for you. It will only work for the first person who found it."

Hans slashed a hand through the air impatiently. "Go on! Hurry up so I don't have to live in this horrid place anymore. And don't make any excuses or I'll know, and everyone will hear about Fritz the child killer."

With a furtive look around, as if there was ever anyone else down by the lake, Hans hurried back up the road to the village. Fritz sighed, folded the parchment into his pocket, and went to get his net.

He tried not to be upset with Hans. Several mornings ago, his father, Jürgen, had been hauled out of the well, his whole body bloated, his skin fish-belly white and marbled with blue veins. The children he had kept under his shop could not say what he had been doing with them, only that he would take one of them away every so often and they would never be seen again. The villagers did not mourn Jürgen; they gave him no burial, instead tossing his body into the forest for the animals. Ulrich was carving a statue in Liesel's likeness which would be mounted near the well. They had found a dress in the well that many now assumed was hers. Her boots were probably at the bottom of the well somewhere. The consensus was she'd died and turned into a warg.

Hans claimed he had not known about the children under the house, and Fritz believed him, but not everyone did. And

Hans had never spent the time or effort to learn his father's trade, so now others in the village were vying to take Jürgen's place as butcher. Hans was alone and, for a while, Fritz had felt bad for him.

That feeling was gone now, and something worse had taken its place.

Fritz got into his little old boat, the one his father had passed on to him after Fritz had helped him build a new one, and rowed out into the lake. Thunder rumbled overhead, but thunder was usually rumbling these days. A light snow dusted the boat. The lake would not freeze, no matter how cold it got. Fritz huddled into his jacket and hat, wishing his gloves were thicker, wondering if he could convince Heike to make him something warmer. She'd been a little distant since she'd gone into the woods to speak to the witch, but maybe she just hadn't been eating enough. Maybe a nice string of salmon . . .

The lake curved to the east and south, and the forest made a tall gray barrier around its shores. Fritz angled the boat east, to a spot where the bank had crumbled and a tree had fallen across the mouth of a small inlet. The tree's roots twisted upward like broken fingers, and its branches made an impassable tangle, but between the two, the trunk slanted at an angle that left Fritz just enough room to scrunch down and guide his boat into the inlet.

The inlet was dark and peaceful, the water lapping gently against the sides of the boat and the banks of the lake. Fritz eased his net over the boat's side and lowered it into the water. The net had a large triangular mouth fastened onto the end of a pole, so he didn't have to get his hands wet hauling it in and out of the water. He waited patiently, not moving, wishing he could see below the iron-gray surface so that he would know if the fish was still here, or if it was purposefully avoiding him.

He had lied to Hans when he'd said the fish would only listen to the person who had first found it. Fritz couldn't read well, and he wasn't good at much else besides fishing, but he wasn't stupid; if Hans knew where to find the fish, Fritz was sure he'd do something terrible with it. There had been a time when Fritz would have told him right away, when he would have been too scared to argue with Hans, when he would have given Hans whatever he wanted, because Hans was his closest friend in the world. But that was before Katrina had died.

There was a tug on the net, and Fritz exhaled and slouched back in relief. He hauled the net out of the water and carefully set it on the floor of the boat. Inside the net was a flounder, flat and round, with two ugly little eyes staring at him from the side of its head. It didn't flop around like other fish, but instead remained still. Its tail curled and slapped once, as if annoyed.

"What does he want *now*?" the flounder asked.

two

Flounders lived in the ocean, not in lakes, which was the first thing Fritz had thought when he'd hauled it out of the water several weeks before. He'd never fished in the ocean, but his grandfather had, and his father had told him about the types of fish that lived there. He had stared at the flounder hanging on the end of his line, and the flounder had stared back, and then Fritz had begun the task of unhooking it. What a catch! His father would be very interested to see this, and to know that the flounder had been inside the dark little inlet with the felled tree blocking the entrance. Like the lake creature that had washed up years ago, the flounder was something that wasn't where it was supposed to be.

Then the hook had come out of its mouth, and the flounder had said, "Thanks for stabbing me in the cheek, you bastard."

Fritz, who had a habit of giving fish voices when he was by himself on the lake, had paused and wondered when he'd started making *angry* fish voices. He usually made them nice. Happy Mr. Fish, happy to feed the village.

"Yes, it's *me*," the flounder had said, slapping its tail against the boat. "Listen, if you promise not to eat me, I'll give you a wish. Well, you'll have to answer a riddle first, but I'll make it easy."

"How can you speak?" Fritz asked, still not sure if he had fallen asleep and was dreaming.

"How do you think? It's magic. And I'm human, too, so if you eat me, you're committing cannibalism. Know that before you make any decisions here today."

"You're a magic fish," Fritz said, "and you can grant me a wish."

"I'm a magic *human*," the fish said, "and I can grant you *many* wishes, but I need you to help me. I need you to wish for me to be human again."

"Oh. But you're magic."

"Yes."

"And I can wish for anything?"

"*Yes.*"

"Can I have time to think about it?"

"I—I suppose? Why do you need time to think about it? You must listen to me: I have been trapped this way for many years, I haven't seen family or friends, I can't even go out into the lake for fear I'll be eaten by a larger fish or pulled up by a fisherman and ignored when I beg for mercy. . . ."

"I need to think about it," Fritz said, scooping the flounder up off the deck. "But I'll be back."

"Oh, fine! But next time, bring a net instead!" It was the last thing the flounder said before Fritz slipped it back into the water.

Fritz had then rowed calmly back to the dock, his strokes slow and even, gaze fixed in the middle distance. He expected the encounter to fade in his mind like a dream upon waking, but it didn't. It stayed fixed there as he tethered the boat to the dock, took his tools into the hut, and then sprinted full tilt into town.

He ran straight across the square, slipped around the butcher's shop, and knocked furiously on the cottage door until Hans appeared. His hair was awry and his eyes half-lidded, a scowl forming.

"Oh," Fritz said, "it's early."

"Did you wake me up to tell me it's early?" Hans asked.

"N-no. No. I found something."

He told the story quickly, not even stopping to think about why he had come straight to Hans, or why Hans was the one he was telling. Later this would haunt him, but at the time it seemed obvious, even logical. Hans was his best friend. You told your best friends about the strange and interesting things that happened to you, because you wanted them to share in the adventure.

Hans leaned on the doorframe and said, "You're saying . . . in the lake . . . there's an enchanted fish that grants wishes?"

"Y-yes."

"Okay, so prove it. Have it grant a wish."

"Like what?"

"Like *what*?" Hans sneered. "You really don't have any imagination, do you, Fritz? Think something up. Like . . . wish for the redberries to bear fruit. Except not the ones close to town—in case it's some kind of trap, you want to keep any magic far away from where you live. Wish for the berry bushes past the river to produce."

"You think that'll—" Fritz began, but Hans shut the door.

Hans didn't believe him then, but Fritz rowed right back out onto the lake—then had to turn back to quickly fix up one of his father's old nets on a short pole—and to the inlet. Hands shaking, he lowered the net into the water. It wasn't under the surface long enough for him to start worrying about whether the fish had been real before there was a tug against his hands and he lifted the net to find the flounder there, looking ugly and annoyed.

"I'm ready to make a wish," Fritz said.

"I want you to promise me first that you'll use the next wish to turn me human again," said the flounder.

"How many wishes do I get?"

"As many as the riddles you answer correctly, at least until my magic runs out. But who knows when that will be, and let us pray it never happens."

"Okay," said Fritz, "I'll use a wish to make you human again."

"I will regret this," replied the flounder. "Please don't wish for anything stupid. Here is your riddle: *We lap, we whisper, we crash, we roll. Our mother wind births us each differently. What are we?*"

"Waves," Fritz said, without hesitation.

The flounder sighed. Fritz felt a moment of annoyance— even a fish thought he wasn't smart enough to answer a riddle as simple as that! "Go ahead," said the flounder.

"I wish the redberries were ripe on the bushes again, but only on the bushes west of the Idle River Bridge."

The flounder was completely still. Then, a second later, it flipped its tail and said, "Done. Your berries are on their bushes. Now, if you'll wish me back—"

"I have to check first," said Fritz. "To make sure it really happened."

"You can't take my word for it?"

"I won't be long. I'll come back tomorrow."

The flounder began to struggle in its net. "Boy, do you have any idea how long I have—"

Fritz quickly dipped the flounder back into the water. "Back tomorrow!"

His father was home by the time he made it to shore, but later that afternoon he was able to come up with an excuse to go into the village, where he found Hans and Liesel walking down the path from the Klein's farm, where they sometimes went to be alone. Liesel split off and hurried through the field before Fritz reached them.

He told Hans about the berries. Hans said, "Okay, go run and pick some, and then we'll know for sure."

Fritz had thought Hans might go with him, but he didn't; he probably had more important things to do than run down the road checking on out-of-season berry bushes. But Fritz also couldn't be gone from home that long or his father would notice. So he waited until that night, when his father went to bed—always early these days, asleep with the sun—before he ventured down the west road. He didn't take a light with him, because the blue-flame lanterns along the road were always lit, and he didn't want to draw attention to himself. He jogged the whole way to the bridge; the forest made his hair stand on end. When he reached his destination, he didn't have to search long: right off the road was a loaded redberry bush, as fresh and green as if it was high summer. He pocketed a handful, his fingers shaking in his gloves, and took off back for the village, all exhaustion forgotten. The fish could grant wishes.

He went straight to Hans—no one else would believe him, even if they saw the berries, he was sure. He wasn't sure how he was going to wake Hans without also waking Jürgen, but when he arrived at the butcher's shop, there was a lantern flickering out back, and he found Hans at the large wooden tray he used for bleaching bones. Hans was bent over the tray, arranging bones of all sizes. The sunlight over Greymist Fair was rarely very strong, but Hans was patient.

Fritz approached him cautiously, and Hans glanced up as if he'd known Fritz would appear at that moment. Fritz said nothing, just held out the berries. Hans stared at them. Plucked one from Fritz's hand. Ate it.

Then he looked at Fritz, eyes dark in the lantern light, and said, "Let's make another wish."

three

The second wish had been much more public. Hans had wanted elk to stampede through the village. Several would be killed, giving his father more meat to butcher and sell and giving Hans more bones to pick through. Fritz, entranced by this magic, had mostly worried about how to form the wish to ensure no one was injured in the stampede, but the flounder had bigger problems.

"You promised you'd use this one to turn me human again," the fish said, wriggling in agitation. "You'll be going against your word, boy."

"No, I won't," Fritz said. "I promised I would use a wish to turn you human again; I didn't promise I would use my *next* wish to turn you human again. And I will! I will use a wish to turn you human again, but if I turn you human now, you'll probably run off."

"I'm not granting you any more wishes until you turn me human."

"Okay, well . . ." Fritz thought for a moment. "Then I guess you'll stay in this inlet, and I'll cover the entrance with even more branches to hide it so no one ever comes back here again, and you can stay a flounder forever."

This prompted the flounder's most intense bout of flailing, along with a string of very human curses that had Fritz's ears turning pink. When the flounder at last seemed to tire, it stared up at him with its beady little eyes and said, *"Fine."*

And so there had been a stampede of elk, and Fritz hadn't even been there to see it, but he saw the results. With the recent death of Tomas, and Heike's journey into the woods, not to mention the strange and worsening weather they'd experienced, much of the village was in a haze of excitement and suspicion. Fritz realized too late that the stampede of elk was, to many of the villagers, another sign that Death had killed the witch and now reigned over the woods, as Heike had said. So close to Yule, with snow already dusting the ground and more promised by the darkening clouds, everyone should have been preparing for twelve days of feasting, gift giving, and celebration. Instead, they were more frightened of the woods than ever and looking for someone to blame.

Hans had been placated by the elk for a while. But then his father had died and been outed as the murderer of children, and he was alone, and he'd come and found Fritz and asked to be made king of Greymist Fair. No one in town liked Hans all that much, but Fritz wasn't sure they liked *him*, either, and so he didn't know whose word they would take if Hans decided to tell his lies. Hans as king probably wouldn't be all that bad. He would get bored with it quickly, Fritz was sure. Absolutely sure.

So, Fritz rowed to the inlet the fourth time, netted the flounder, and pulled it up into his little boat. "What does he want *now*?" the flounder had asked, and Fritz could not tell it. He was sure if he said it, the flounder wouldn't give him the riddle.

"It's freezing up here, pock face," said the flounder irritably. "Let's get this over with. *Some call him ugly, some call him annoying, all call him friendless. He doesn't even realize. Who is he?*"

"He's you," Fritz said, surprised to find he was annoyed that the riddle wasn't harder. If it had been difficult enough so that he couldn't solve it, then Hans wouldn't get to be king.

You could wish for something else, Fritz thought. *You don't have to do what Hans wants.*

But then who would talk to Fritz?

The flounder looked surprised, as much as it was possible for a flounder to look surprised. "I—well—I suppose that—it's not *technically* incorrect—the way I look now and—do you think I'm annoying?"

"Was that not the answer?"

"No! The answer was—ugh—the answer was *you*, yes, but *you* you, not *me* you! But even so—I didn't always look like this, you know! I look much better when I'm not a fish!"

Confused, Fritz stared at the flounder. "I'm sure you're very . . . handsome? As a human. But you're saying I answered correctly?"

"I *suppose*—although I'm not—Evren would still be my friend, wherever he is. Evren's not still in the town, is he?"

"I don't know who Evren is."

"Of course you don't. He left. Probably thought I ran off without him. Oh, fine! Make your wish and leave me alone!"

Fritz made the wish. The flounder went still for a very long time, and then seemed to deflate on the bottom of the boat.

"Oh, what have you done, pock face?" the flounder asked tiredly. "What have you done for this boy you think is your friend?"

four

Fritz found out what he'd done as soon as he reached the shore.

The wind was bitingly cold and thick flakes of snow had begun to fall, turning the world hazy white. He stumbled up the hill from the dock, hoping to get inside and start a fire before his fingers were too numb to hold the flint, but where he should have seen the hut huddled against the trees, there were only a few tumbled walls disappearing beneath a veil of frost. He stepped carefully closer, trying to find his bed beneath the walls, trying to find their cook pots, their tools, but the remains of the structure was a blackened heap, long since ruined.

His father had been inside the hut when Fritz set out on the lake. Where was he now? Fritz pulled his coat tighter, his hat farther down on his head, and hurried up the road toward the village.

He saw the turrets of the castle rising over the treetops long before he reached the village square. There was no castle in Greymist Fair, had never *been* a castle in Greymist Fair, yet here one was, a small castle for a small king. It sat on the eastern overlook where Greymist Manor had been all Fritz's life, roosting like a dank gray gargoyle. A flag fluttered from its towers, a black eagle on a gold field. Lights danced in its slitted windows; torches dotted its battlements.

The village was silent. The snow made it eerily so. Fritz passed deserted cottages, many collapsed, decaying, as if they had been abandoned for years. He forgot he was looking for his father and began looking for *anyone*, anyone at all, to ask what had happened here. Where was everyone? The swirling snow made any unfamiliar shape appear to be a person until Fritz looked a little closer, and then it was only the open door of Johanna and Dagny's bakery, or the lonely well, or the tumbled stone wall outside the inn. The inn itself was a black husk; it had clearly burned down. Fritz froze when he saw it. The chill seemed to seep into his lungs. Someone had torched the inn.

I want that dirty innkeep as my whipping boy.

Fritz spun and squinted up through the snow at the looming castle. Hans had wanted all the villagers as his servants. What would they need their own homes for if they were all serving the king?

The air seemed to get colder as Fritz, huddled against the

snow, made his way up the rise to the castle. His toes were long since numb, and he could hardly keep his eyes open. He needed to get warm.

Up close, the castle wasn't much larger than the manor had been, nor did it look much like Fritz thought a castle should; it was as if the manor house had simply been altered. There was no castle wall, no moat, no drawbridge, no court-yard, nothing that other castles had in all the stories. There was the facade of the manor house, and the house itself had been extended back, given an extra two stories, and grown towers that cleared the treetops. Fritz couldn't see anyone walking the battlements. The manor's front doors had been extended upward, and a man with a very large dog sat in front of them, tending a small fire.

"Gottfried!" Fritz stumbled up to the fire. The Duke, tight against Gottfried's side, bared his fangs and let out a warning growl. Gottfried's dark eyes looked out from under his hat.

"Young Fritz," said Gottfried. His voice was muffled by the thick scarf over his mouth. "Thought you were inside already. How'd you get out?"

"I—don't know," Fritz said, feeling out of his depth. Gottfried was never this subdued, and Fritz had never heard The Duke growl. "I'm looking for my father. Is he inside?"

"Everyone's inside. You best be, too. Go on now." Gottfried motioned his head toward the doors.

Fritz edged his way around the slight warmth of the fire and hurried toward the oak doors. The Duke watched him, hackles raised. Fritz had to use his entire body to shove one of the doors open, then fell onto the smooth stone floor of the entrance hall.

Walls stretched upward to a dark, arched ceiling. Tapestries hung along both sides told different stories. On the left: a beautiful girl longed to have magic and was chased through the forest by shadows and killed. On the right: a boy that resembled Hans also longed to have magic, but he made it out of the forest and obtained magic and became a king. Warmth and music came through the doors at the end of the entrance hall.

In the huge great hall, roaring fires blazed in pits at either end of long feasting tables. The villagers of Greymist Fair filled the seats, many wearing servant's livery or the gray-washed winter garb of hunters and craftspeople. A small band played near the bonfire on the far side of the room, closest to the wide dais with its tall golden throne. On the throne sat Hans. A jewel-encrusted crown perched on his white-blond hair, and he scanned disinterestedly a plate of charred meat proffered by a servant. With a jolt, Fritz realized the servant was Wenzel.

Hans knocked the plate out of Wenzel's hands and said,

"Look how clumsy you are, Grub. Get on your knees and pick it up."

Fritz couldn't see Wenzel's expression, but the set of his shoulders was stiff as he kneeled on the floor.

Fritz couldn't breathe. He'd assumed, when he had made the wish, that the change would come gradually. Hans would be made king, then the villagers might start serving him, then he would probably move into the manor, but life would largely go on like it had before. But no—the world had changed instantly, yanked out from under Fritz's feet. This was not the Greymist Fair he knew. This was not the way things were supposed to be.

He found his father skulking near the firepit closest to the door, spooning some kind of foul-looking mash into his mouth. Fritz hurried over to him, kneeled by his side.

"Father," he said, "what happened to our home?"

Falk turned dull eyes on his son. "We sleep here now," he grunted. "What were *you* doing at the lake? You'll be whipped for fishing."

"Whipped for fishing? But why—"

A heavy hand landed on Fritz's shoulder. Ulrich, the carpenter, stood over him with a stony but sorry look on his face. "Enough talk, boy. Come along. The king wishes to speak with you."

Ulrich gently helped Fritz to his feet—Fritz was taller, but Ulrich had easily sixty extra pounds of muscle—and marched him toward the throne. Hans, previously entertained watching Wenzel crawl around the floor for scraps of food, turned his attention to Fritz and smiled. He waved Ulrich off.

"Hello, friend," Hans said. "Look at what we've accomplished!"

He gestured toward the great hall. Fritz looked over at the sunken-eyed villagers, their small and unappetizing portions of gray nameless mash. Several cast glances at him, but quickly looked away. If the scene had been told to Fritz in a story, he would have said it was unbelievable. It was almost comical, how downtrodden and miserable they seemed.

"Did you ban fishing?" Fritz asked, his mind blank of any other questions.

"Of course I did," said Hans. "Couldn't have anyone else finding our benefactor, could I? Don't worry, you can still go out. I was thinking you should move the fish here, to the castle. It's magical, so the move shouldn't kill it. I'll have Grub dig a little pool for it." He shoved his heel into Wenzel's side, catching Wenzel by surprise and knocking him off the dais, onto his back. Hans laughed. Wenzel flashed a dark look at him and rolled onto his side.

Fritz quickly scanned the room for Heike. If there was anyone who would know what to do, it would be her. She was brave enough to go into the forest alone, to speak to Death. She could handle Hans. But she was nowhere to be found.

Fritz stayed where he was, pinned in place with uncertainty. He lowered his voice. "About the fish—after this last wish, he seemed tired. Very tired. I think this one took more out of him than usual. I don't know how much more he'll be able to do."

"It's *magic*," Hans snapped. "A magic fish doesn't just *run out of magic*. It was probably tricking you to keep you from making more wishes. Can't you even see through a ruse as simple as that?"

I can't see through much of anything, Fritz thought, hating himself. What had he done? *What had he done?*

Plate and food recovered, Wenzel stood and returned to Hans's side. But Hans was visibly upset now, and Wenzel's approach only redirected his anger. Hans twisted in his seat, grabbed the plate, and threw it down the middle aisle between the long tables. Then, standing, he rounded on Wenzel and slapped him so hard the sound made the musicians grind to a halt and all conversation in the hall cease. "Pig!" Hans yelled. "Useless grub! Now you've thrown food all over the room. Did it make you feel better? Do you feel like you have taught me some lesson?" Another slap, this one to the other cheek. Wenzel kept his eyes down, his face expressionless. His hands were balled into white-knuckled fists at his sides. "Ulrich! Godric! Come take him to the post. I think it's been too long."

The carpenter and the blacksmith lumbered to the dais to collect Wenzel, who shrugged off their light holds and stared, unblinking, at Hans as he stepped down to the floor. He held his head high as they passed between the tables and out of the hall.

Hans turned back to Fritz, grinning. "This is the strangest thing that has ever happened to me! I know the magic only just changed things, and yet I also remember always being king, I remember what I did as king yesterday and the day before. No one else has *any idea* that this is all new! Can you think of anything better?"

Fritz glanced at the tables, the villagers carefully bent over their bowls, their conversations quiet. It would be better if they didn't all look like beaten animals. It would be better if the musicians weren't sweating into their instruments, eyes haunted, like a wrong note might get them killed. If they had no memory of how things were before Fritz made the wish, then what *did* they remember?

"Come on, let's not keep Grub waiting too long." Hans hopped up from his seat, snatching his crown as it slid off his slick hair, and wheeled Fritz toward a door behind the throne. Beyond it was a stone hallway that led to a staircase that led them up and up, four or even five floors, Fritz wasn't sure. Hans seemed to know where he was going. Did he know what kind of king he was? Did he know what he'd done to the villagers to make them act like that in his presence?

At the top of the staircase they passed down another, narrower hallway and came to an iron-banded door, standing open. Ulrich and Godric stood on either side, their faces impassive. Hans and Fritz walked between them and into the bedroom beyond, and the two large men looked down on them with coldness. Hans turned and said, "You may go now." He waited until both men had disappeared down the hallway to close the door.

The bedroom was huge and ornate. There was a fireplace, lit, next to a plush sitting area where tea steamed in porcelain cups on a silver tray. There was a four-poster bed draped with dark silks, the sheets still rumpled. A stained-glass window looked out on the snowy night. Across the room, the bones of small animals were displayed in large shadowboxes on the wall, arranged so that they might form full skeletons. In the center of the room was a thick wooden beam running from floor to ceiling, and facing it, his hands bound just above his head, was Wenzel.

Fritz's blood ran cold. He had never seen a whipping—there was no physical punishment for crimes in Greymist Fair—but he knew what the setup would look like. Wenzel's forehead was pressed to the wooden post, the firelight glinting off the dark wave of his hair. He was still clothed, thankfully; maybe that meant the whipping wouldn't be as bad as Fritz feared.

"Don't look so dour," Hans said. Fritz jumped, unaccustomed to Hans reading his expressions, but Hans wasn't speaking to him. Or Wenzel.

Between two large shadowboxes, on a thin-legged chair, sat Heike.

five

Heike was pale, her hands fisted in her skirts, gold eyes glowing with hatred. She had been so still and so quiet Fritz hadn't seen her. Why was she here? Why had Hans *known* she was here?

Hans went to the bed and took down a short leather whip. A thin blade gleamed on its end. He stroked its length, smiling, and cracked it experimentally in the air. Wenzel's hands tightened on his metal cuffs, the muscles in his forearms bulging.

"You're going to have to get yourself a new shirt after this, Grub," Hans said. "Didn't Heike make that one for you? That's too bad. She only works for me now."

Fritz opened his mouth to protest at the same time Hans snapped his arm out. The whip flashed. Wenzel cried out in surprise and staggered against the post as a slash opened in the back of his shirt and crimson stained the white linen. Heike jolted to her feet but moved no further, her lips pressed white, her eyes wide with fury. Hans giggled. *Giggled*.

"It's not a deep cut, but how effective!" he said, marveling at the whip. "How many lashes before there isn't any skin left to cut? The line is so thin—surely it would be hundreds?"

"What *for*?" Fritz's voice was high. "Hans, what is this for? What did he do? You can't just—j-just *whip* people!"

Hans's glee curdled into petulance. "Of course I can. I'm the king. Or did you think we were somewhere else?"

In some world that doesn't exist anymore?

"Yes, b-but you hurt him, look at his back!"

"*You hurt him*," Hans mocked. "You want to be next? I'll tie you to that pole instead if you want to take his place. Shut up and let me have my fun. Grub has annoyed me for long enough. Why should *he* be happy? He has nothing. He *is* nothing. Hear that, Grub?" He flicked the whip lightly at the back of Wenzel's legs, making Wenzel tense. Then Hans leaned to look around Wenzel at Heike. "Same goes for you. I'll whip a friend of the old witch, don't think I won't. My magic is stronger than anything the witch ever had."

Fritz, frozen in an unreality he couldn't fathom, almost missed it when Hans lifted the whip a second time.

"Stop!" Fritz caught Hans's arm and grabbed the whip. They struggled for possession, dragging each other across the floor. Hans smashed Fritz against the footboard of the bed, but Fritz kept his hold, and they both toppled over onto the sheets. Hans shoved his knees into Fritz's stomach, crushing the air out of him, and released the whip with one hand to pound his fist into Fritz's eye. Stunned, Fritz lost his grip. Hans reared back, whip raised, with a triumphant, *"HA!"*

The bed warmer, filled with hot coals from the fire, slammed into the side of Hans's head. The force threw him over the edge of the bed. He thudded to the floor and began screaming.

Heike dropped the bed warmer with a clang and spun to Wenzel. She tore the red ribbon out of her hair, releasing her braid, and wound it through the manacle on Wenzel's wrist. She started sawing back and forth.

"That's a r-ribbon," Fritz yelled, scrambling to his feet. "It's useless."

"Shut up," Heike spat. "I'm not very good at this yet and it can be hard to make it work. This isn't what you think, Fritz. I don't know how, but Hans got into some magic and made himself king—"

"H-how?" Fritz moved around the pole to meet her eye.

"Because it's magic that made everyone forget," she said, "but I don't think it can make me forget. And you?"

"I was the one who made the wish," he said. "It's my fault."

She spared him a quick, cold glance, then returned to her task. "Can you fix it?"

He thought of the tired flounder. "M-maybe."

"Then we have to try." There was a soft *clink*, and Wenzel's right wrist came free of the manacle. "Watch out. Move." Heike came around to the other side of the post and wound her ribbon through the other manacle, sawing again. Fritz watched as the red silk wore away the iron in visible shavings, like scaling a fish. Magic. Heike had magic, somehow. There was another soft *clink* as the last bit of iron lost its hold, and Wenzel leaned against the pole and withdrew his hand.

"Can we get out of here, please?" he asked, grimacing and glancing at Hans, who was unconscious on the floor. A sheen of sweat covered his face. Heike gently took Wenzel's arm and led him toward the door.

"Heike," Wenzel said as they crossed the threshold, "they'll be coming up soon—they'll kill Fritz, too, if they think he's Hans's friend."

"I'm not his friend," Fritz said, taking Wenzel's other arm. Then, backtracking, "W-wait, *who* will kill me?"

Heike blew a lock of hair out of her face. "The villagers. They're planning a coup. They're going to throw Hans out into the snow. They saw you with him in the great hall, and Ulrich and Godric saw you come here with Wenzel. They *might* listen to us if we tell them you helped us escape, but they're all very angry, and I don't know if we can convince them." She didn't say the rest, but Fritz understood. *Or if we want to try.*

Fritz didn't blame her; he didn't entirely feel like he deserved to get out of the mess he'd made. All he'd wanted was to escape Hans's lies, and he'd gotten tangled up in them anyway.

"Do either of you know how to get out of here?" Heike asked. "Everyone except me seems to know where things are around here."

"N-no idea," Fritz said, feeling even worse about himself.

"Door on the third-floor landing," Wenzel said. "There's a corridor and a back staircase that leads down to the servant's quarters. But where are we going?"

"First, we're getting out of here," Heike said. The murmur of angry voices and the scrape of leather and metal on stone was echoing up the stairs. "And on the way, Fritz is going to tell us how he made this happen, and how he can change things back to the way they were."

They crept down the stairs and pushed through the door on the third-floor landing. In a low voice, Fritz told them the story of finding the flounder and testing its magic, and making Hans's wish and returning to the village to find it as it was now. By that point they were several flights down a narrow servant's stair and coming to the ground floor.

"You're saying none of this is real," Wenzel said, staring hard at Fritz while Heike peeked around the corner to make sure their way was clear, "and it's all because you answered a riddle from a fish in the lake and made a wish?"

"It's *real*; it's just not *right*. If I can get back to the fish, I can wish it back to normal."

Heike motioned to them. They emerged in a guardroom, dark but dry, lit only by the torch at the door. They found a heavy coat and hat, which Heike immediately pulled on, though they were too big for her.

"I can't find any others," Wenzel said. "We'll have to go look somewhere else."

"No." Heike pulled her hood up and arranged the scarf over her face. "You're hurt. Go find Doctor Death, or even Gabi. They'll fix you up. You can't go running around out in the cold with your back cut open."

Wenzel turned a hurt look on her. "But you can't go, either. It's too dangerous. The cold could—or the forest—"

Heike, scanning him, hesitated and then reached out to take his hand. "We won't be in the forest; we'll be on the lake. You're *hurt*. You can barely stand. We have to do this, or the town is going to destroy itself. I know you don't remember, but there is something better than this." Her hand moved up to his cheek and Fritz looked away, very conscious of his own presence. "You never like it when I go, but I always come back to you. I promise this time won't be different. Okay?"

Wenzel muttered, "Okay."

Heike was grabbing Fritz's arm and yanking him toward the guardhouse door. "Let's go," she said. "And I hope you're ready to run."

They were halfway down the rise to the castle when fresh screaming pierced the air.

"Hans woke up," Heike said over the wind. They slouched close together as they jogged through snowdrifts.

Fritz glanced back at the castle, terrified. The torch in his hand wavered. "What will they do with him? They clearly hate him. Will they really—really k-kill him?"

Heike thought for a moment, then said, "No. I think they'll send him into the forest."

"Isn't that killing him?"

"Only if he fears Death."

Fritz didn't understand this, but his teeth were freezing

and it was making his head pound, so he closed his mouth and stopped talking. Something about Heike had changed since her journey into the woods. She'd gotten older, somehow. She saw things the rest of them didn't.

The snow was already piled high, turning Greymist Fair into a field of white hills that glimmered faintly under a bright moon, visible now in a gap between the clouds. Fritz and Heike ran when they could, taking awkward, bowlegged leaps, but by the time they made it to the road to the lake, they were both panting. It didn't feel quite so cold anymore, which Fritz found worrying. His father had always told him that was the time to be afraid, when the cold stopped being cold.

Finally they reached Grey Lake. Clouds had again obscured the moon, and the lake was a dark abyss before them. Fritz kicked his way to the snow-laden dock and found his little boat, flipped over on the shore, covered.

"We'll have to clear this off," he said, holding out the torch to Heike. "I can push most of it off the hull, then we can row to the inlet—"

"Fritz," Heike said, taking the torch and looking off the side of the dock. Fritz followed her gaze. There was a powdering of snow on the surface of the water. Holding on to a post, Fritz lowered his leg over the side of the dock and kicked at the snow. Below was an icy sheet, and beneath that, darkness. When he set his foot down, the ice held. He kicked at it. The impact reverberated up his leg, and he'd only managed to scuff the surface.

Pulling himself back up, Fritz hurried to the end of the dock and leaned over, holding the torch out. A layer of snow covered everything as far as the light could reach. He paused there, breathless, until the clouds shifted and the moon emerged again. The lake glowed in the night, a great disc of haunting blue-white bordered by a black wall of trees.

Grey Lake had frozen.

six

Heike ignored Fritz's protestations—"But the lake *never* freezes!"—and forced him to put together a list of things they would need, which was short. Something to break the ice, and his net. Heike unearthed his net from under the snowed-in boat while Fritz searched the ruins of the hut for his father's iron fire poker. He found it only after shoving nearly a whole wall out of the way, ripping his right glove and slashing his skin open in the process.

Tools in hand, he led Heike out onto the ice. They stayed close to the shore in case the ice grew thin, but he never heard so much as a creak beneath the snow cover. His eyes watered; the wind had picked up, and they were walking directly into it. He tried to stay in front of Heike to block her from the worst. Reaching the inlet was a blessing; they ducked under the fallen tree and were immediately protected by the forest around them. Face chapped and numb, Fritz stepped out into the middle of the inlet, testing the ice.

"I don't understand how this happened," he said. "I was just here, and the lake was the same as always. It's never frozen before, and now it's completely solid only a few hours after I last saw it."

"Fritz," Heike said, sounding tired, "I don't believe you're as simpleminded as Hans thinks you are, and I need you to keep up now. This weather isn't just weather. The forest isn't just forest. Your fish isn't just a fish. We have passed from the world of reason; this is the world of magic. I need you to know where you are. Do you?"

The torchlight cast Heike's face in gold and bronze. She didn't seem cold at all, and she looked at him with a steadiness that he'd rarely seen from adults, and never from his own father. He felt so small, so lost, he may as well have been a child again, crying when he wandered too far down the shore and lost sight of the hut. Right now, there was no time for crying or for questioning. There was only time for doing.

"I do," he said. Heike nodded. Fritz handed her the torch so he could take the fire poker in both hands and began hacking his way through the ice.

The ice didn't crack, but it did chip away. Fritz was able to carve a hole through the surface to the water beneath, widening it until the mouth of his net would slip through. He threw the fire poker aside and gasped when it tore his glove and some of his skin away with it; his blood had frozen everything together. The gasp chilled his teeth and made him feel as if his skull had frosted over beneath his skin. He took the net from Heike and thrust it through the hole in the ice.

They waited. Fritz kneeled by the hole, net handle in hand and eyes closed, praying nothing had happened to the flounder. His legs were going numb; he wasn't sure he was going to be able to stand up again. There was no sense of anything under the ice except for the gentle ebb and flow of water, and the chill began to seep into the pit of Fritz's stomach.

Then a tug on the net, so subtle it might have been nothing. Fritz opened his eyes, staring down into the dark water. A second tug, harder. He cried out and yanked the net up, hand over hand until he was wedging the curled body of the ugly flounder through the hole and onto the ice.

"'S cold," the flounder said.

"I need another riddle," Fritz said. "I need to put things back the way they were."

"Don't know if I can help you with that," said the flounder. There was something glazed about the flounder's eyes. It lifted the corner of its tail weakly. "I'm about out of magic, I think," the flounder said. "End of the line. That last wish was a big one.

I never actually thought about running out of magic, what it would be like. I guess it means dying. I never thought that it would mean dying. I was really looking forward to being human again."

"You can't grant the wish because you don't have enough magic?" Heike asked.

"Hello. Didn't know there was someone else there."

Fritz shifted the net so the flounder could see Heike.

"Oh—you look like someone I knew once. I gave her a wish. I think she used it to turn me into a fish. It was a long time ago, though, and I probably deserved it. I think I was a bit of an ass."

"You said you don't have enough magic?" Heike asked again.

"I don't think so," said the flounder. "Doesn't it seem a little silly, that you should *run out*? Does everyone who has magic run out of it, or do you think that's just me, maybe? I could see it just being me; I never deserved as much as I had in the first place. What an ass I was."

Heike reached into the net and gently lifted the flounder out, drawing it into her lap, heedless of the icy water that soaked her dress. "What if you borrowed some magic? Could that work?"

The flounder, surprised, paused before answering. "You would do that? Just . . . give it to me?"

"For this, yes," Heike said. "For Greymist Fair. I don't know how much I have, but I can try."

"It might not be good for you."

"We don't have a choice."

"I don't suppose pock face has any magic to contribute?"

Heike glanced at Fritz. "No, I don't think so."

They fell silent, and Fritz had the strangest sensation that they were still communicating somehow, in a way he couldn't even perceive. Watching them, he understood what Heike meant about being in a different world, except he was only living in it *right now*, and they lived in it *always*. It was a world governed not by the laws of nature or reason but by a will of its own, fickle and beautiful and dangerous.

Heike raised her head. The flounder said, "Okay, pock face, here's your riddle. Are you ready? The wording of the wish doesn't have to be so specific—the magic will know what you want."

"B-but," Fritz said, feeling himself slipping from that precipice of adulthood, "I said I would wish you human again."

"Don't worry about that now," said the flounder. "I've been a fish for so long I don't remember what it's like to be human anyway."

"But you'll die."

"We'll all die," said the flounder.

Fritz scrubbed a hand over his face. He had to do this. For Greymist Fair. "Okay. What's the riddle?"

"What leaves you empty and fills you up?"

It was the simplest one yet. Fritz answered, "Home."

The flounder seemed to sink into Heike's dress as the magic took hold.

"I wish Greymist Fair was right again."

There was a silence. A pause. An intake of breath. Both Heike and the fish went very still. Fritz felt nothing but cold. Then the flounder slipped from Heike's hands and onto the ice, and Heike herself slumped sideways.

Fritz leaped up as soon as he saw her, but his frozen knees made him stumble and he fell across the body that lay between them.

"Oh," the body moaned. Fritz pushed himself up. Where the flounder had been, there was now a man in an embroidered coat and tall boots, his dark hair neatly styled and glossy in the torch's light. The man threw a hand over his face and moaned again. "Oh, death! I knew hell would be cold! Even here I can't get warm!"

Fritz rocked back on his heels, dumbfounded. "You aren't in

hell," he said. "You're—I suppose you were the flounder, weren't you? You used up all your magic and now you're human again. But you didn't die."

"Stop lying to me to make me feel better, pock face. I've just *died*, can't you see?"

The man turned his head away, then turned it back, lifting his arm and squinting at Fritz with dark eyes. The flounder hadn't been lying before, Fritz had to admit; he *was* handsome. "Pock face?" said the man. "What are you doing in hell?"

Fritz rolled his eyes and crawled to Heike, who still hadn't moved. She was unconscious, and when Fritz put his ungloved hand to her cheek, she felt hot despite the freezing air. Her color was high and her breaths were short.

"I think there's something wrong with her," Fritz said. "She needs help. And you'll start freezing in those clothes. Help me with her." When the man just stared between the two of them and his own human hands, Fritz said, louder, "Fish brains! We need to get her back to the village so that we can find help!"

That got the man moving. He stood—he was maybe only a hair or two taller than Fritz—and easily scooped Heike off the ice. Rising on unsteady legs, Fritz grabbed his net, the iron poker, and the torch.

Now it was only him and a man who had once been a

flounder, and Heike was looking worse by the second.

You're the reason you're in this mess, said the small voice in his head, the same one that had told him to be friends with Hans because no one else seemed to want to spend time with him.

But there was another voice in his head now, one that felt more like his own, and it was stronger than the first.

This mess is my fault, it said, *and I'm going to clean it up.*

seven

The flounder had told the truth. The magic had known what Fritz wanted. Greymist Fair was right again.

There was no castle, only Greymist Manor up on its rise. The hut by the lake was standing again, albeit under a cover of snow, and the cottages along the road were back in good repair, though dark. All the noise in town, which wasn't much beneath the snow cover, came from the inn. The inn once again watched over the village square like a smiling mother, firelight in its many windows. There was no sign of an angry mob.

Fritz, who had dropped the poker and net at the hut by the lake, pushed his way into the inn. Villagers crowded the inn's common room and staircase, but they squeezed out of the way so the man carrying Heike could sidle through the door. He'd carried Heike the whole way, and though she still looked like she was burning up, the man's lips were blue, his hair now stuck to his forehead with snow and cold sweat.

Cries of alarm went up through the room, and at once they were set upon by Ulrich and Gabi, Dagny and Johanna, and then Falk, who came and took the spent torch from Fritz's hand and then pulled his son into a hug so tight and so unexpected that Fritz froze for a moment in surprise.

"Don't scare me like that, boy," Falk muttered to him. "You'd give your poor mother a heart attack if she were still here, walking around out in the snow like that."

"What happened?" Gabi asked as she pressed a hand to Heike's forehead and brushed the hair from her face. "Where was she? Did Hans do this to her?"

"And who are you?" Ulrich asked the man holding Heike, who was getting some of the color back in his face. "I'll not be having friends of the little king in this inn."

The little king. The villagers remembered. Fritz pulled out of his father's embrace and pushed himself between Ulrich and the man. "He's not with Hans. He helped put things right again. Heike—I think she's in trouble. Where is Doctor Death?"

"Here." Like his namesake, the doctor materialized seemingly from nowhere, looming at the bottom of the stairs. His face was gaunt and expressionless as he looked down at Heike. "Bring her up."

They hurried upstairs, where Doctor Death had them place Heike in one of the empty rooms of the inn. The doctor ordered them out, but before they could go, the door opened and Wenzel forced his way past Ulrich. His shirt was open, and his torso was bandaged.

"What happened?" he demanded. "Is she okay? Is—" Wenzel saw Heike on the bed and went ashen. "She's not—?"

"She lives," said the doctor, "but I must work. All of you, out."

Fritz and the man stepped into the deserted second-floor hallway. Ulrich returned to grab Wenzel and forced him back into the room next door, where Fritz could hear them arguing.

Fritz sank against the wall, exhausted. The man who had been a flounder stood over him, looking dazed. Eventually he sank down next to Fritz.

"What's your name, fish brain?" Fritz asked.

"Prince Altan," the man said. "I came here from far away. I didn't think I would ever see my home again. Maybe it's gone now. Maybe I'm not a prince anymore." He looked sideways. "What's yours, pock face?"

"Fritz."

"And what's the name of the girl in that room, and the boy in the other?"

"The girl is Heike. The boy is Wenzel."

Prince Altan seemed to consider this, then nodded slowly. "She ended up looking a lot like her mother. And Wenzel—not a bad name, for this place. So much changed. I suppose it's been probably seventeen, eighteen years since I was last here?"

"How old were you then? Five?"

"Add twenty," said the prince.

"You aren't older than twenty-five *now*."

The prince gave him a look, and Fritz shook his head. He knew better. Magic.

"You think you're really out of magic?" Fritz asked.

"I think so," the prince said. "At least, I'm out of the kind I can grant. But maybe that's not permanent. Magic is strange, especially here."

"Do you know what happened to Heike?"

"No idea. But she did give a lot of herself to make that wish work."

Fritz put his head in his hands. "I hope she doesn't die." *It'll be my fault, and there's nothing I can do to fix it.*

The prince took Fritz's wrists and lowered his hands. Fritz looked up in surprise.

"I may not look much older than you," the prince said,

"but I had a long time to think about things in that lake, and you need to listen to me now. We all make mistakes. The good people try to fix them. Sometimes you can't fix them, and you have to live with what happens. Then you just pray to all the gods you know that you don't have to live with it alone."

"That's what got me into all of this," Fritz said. "Not wanting to be alone."

"Like I said, we all make mistakes. Looking for someone to share your time with wasn't a mistake, but the choice of person was. And now you've learned from it, and you'll do better next time." Prince Altan paused, sat back, put a hand on Fritz's shoulder. This time, the touch didn't surprise Fritz. "Let's make another deal. A better one."

"No magic involved?"

"No magic." The prince smiled. "I don't have anyone in Greymist Fair. I'd like to go home eventually, but I'll be here at least through winter. I could use a friend."

Fritz thought at first it was just a gesture. A consolation, the kind that could be bestowed by the more beautiful, the more fortunate, on the less. But then he remembered the riddle he'd answered before he'd wished for Hans to be king. *Some call him ugly, some call him annoying, all call him friendless. He doesn't even realize. Who is he?*

"Your riddles," Fritz said, "Were you the one who determined if the answer was right, or did the magic do that?"

"No," said the prince. "I decided."

Fritz nodded. "I could use a friend, too."

DOCTOR
DEATH

one

One day a man met Death on the road. The man was accompanied by his twelve children; Death was alone, as they often were. The man had never seen Death before, but Death was recognizable to anyone, and the man was instantly afraid.

"Please," said the man, "I cannot die yet; I have twelve children to care for, you see, and to take me would be to kill them as well. You cannot be so cruel as to kill twelve children before they've had a chance to live."

"I do not want to kill you," said Death. "I am lonely and looking for companionship. Would you be willing to part with one of your children? You have so many."

The man quailed, and his children quailed behind him. "I could not bear to let you kill even one. They are children, they are *my* children, and I love them all dearly."

"I will not kill the child," Death said, pleading now. "If the dead could be my companions, I would never be lonely. The child will live and will stay by my side always. They will be well cared for, educated, and will travel to see the world. I will give the child more than you ever could, and they will never know hunger or disease. Will you give one of your children such a wonderful life?"

The man, hearing this, did not find it to be such a horrible proposition after all. He had trouble providing for his twelve children, even now that the oldest of them were able to work, and there was always the threat of a deadly illness or starvation. Life as a companion of Death had to be better than no life at all.

"I will give you my youngest," said the man, "if you swear to me that no harm will come to him."

"I swear," said Death, solemn and truthful. "And you will not see me again until the day your life is to end."

And so the man relinquished his youngest child, an infant in a tight-wrapped bundle, into the hands of Death. Death, taking the small, warm thing, cradled the sleeping boy closely and smiled down on him. From a pocket, Death drew out a sprig of yellow linden blooms and tucked it into the child's blanket.

"His name is Luther," said the man.

Death nodded once, then wrapped the boy in the shadowy folds of their cloak and disappeared.

two

Luther grew up without a mother or a father. Death taught him the ways of the world, and that was enough. He attended schools in the world's greatest cities, filled his mind with the knowledge of people and places his eleven siblings—of whom he had no knowledge, because Death did not find it pertinent—could not imagine. When he had questions, he asked Death. When he needed help, he went to Death. He could not imagine his life without Death in it.

As a young boy he had big hands and feet, and his body hardly seemed to be able to keep up to its own growth. He had straw-like hair he kept cut short or pushed back because he didn't like the feeling of it over his ears or in his eyes. His eyes were pale as slush, and when he caught sight of himself in the mirror, he sometimes jumped at the piercing stare of his own reflection. He dressed in black because Death dressed in black.

He grew into his hands and feet. As he passed into adulthood, he became tall and stern looking, and he found most people listened when he spoke, which wasn't often. Death prompted him to pursue medicine in his studies so that they could spend more time together, and Luther took it up with gusto. As soon as he completed his schooling, he began his rounds from one village to the next, from city to city, country to country. He enjoyed diagnosing illnesses in people and righting them. He liked making others feel better, giving them hope when they thought all was lost. But soon into his career he realized what his close link to Death truly meant in his practice, and it changed the way he viewed everything.

When a patient was going to die, Death appeared at the foot of their sickbed. Only Luther could see Death, and Death would not speak to him at these times. It was a moment they shared, a moment only they understood. Death was here to take. Luther had to let go.

He could not tell his patients this, so he went through the motions of trying to save them, knowing it was in vain.

Soon, word got ahead of him. When Luther visited, you could discover if you were going to die if you could catch his expression right as he entered the room, when he looked to the end of your bed. The doctor could *see* death in the room, the rumors claimed, as some unearthly manifestation, and his stoic face would break into momentary sadness. So that was what they began to call him: Doctor Death.

Doctor Death knew who could be saved and who could not. Patients began outright asking him if death stood at the foot of their beds, and the doctor began answering. Some accepted this sentence and passed into Death's hands willingly. Others demanded the doctor do whatever he could to save them. He would perform every treatment at his disposal, which he knew would not save them, and he never mentioned to anyone the one thing he knew *would* save them.

On his person he carried the sprig from a linden tree, with its little yellow flowers, that had been alive and in bloom since he was a child. Death had told him to keep it with him at all times because linden was the guardian of life, and even Death could not break its power. The doctor knew if he bestowed this sprig on a person marked by Death, he could save them. But he never did. All people come to Death eventually; that was the way of things. But if the doctor remained alive, he could at least help those who were not yet marked.

So the linden blooms remained hidden on his person for all his travels, across the world and back, as he saved souls and lost them and became a wandering myth, someone others saw or whispered about but never knew. He neither liked nor disliked his life: he was there for a purpose, and with Death by his side, he performed it.

Then a day came when he traveled a road he had never been down before. The road led into a dark forest, and in this place, he felt Death more strongly than he ever had before.

"Do you know this forest?" he asked Death.

Death, who was never present in person but always seemed to hover on the edges of the doctor's vision, replied, "This is my home."

Luther had never had a home, and had never thought of Death having one, either. He walked on, following a line of iron lampposts along the side of the road, until the trees parted and a village appeared.

"I didn't know there was a village in this forest," said the doctor.

Death did not reply, and the doctor realized with a jolt that Death was no longer on the edge of his vision. It was as if Death would not leave the trees.

In all his travels, the doctor had never been anywhere Death would not go. Intrigued, he started down into the village to see if there was anyone he could help.

three

Greymist Fair had an apothecary and several residents skilled in herbal medicines and basic first aid, but no trained doctors. Nor did any doctors visit regularly with the traveling merchants who came through. Doctor Death, therefore, made an impression as he swept through town. He stopped first at the inn to rent a room, and while there diagnosed one of the kindly old innkeepers with nearsightedness. Then he went to see Lord Greymist in his manor on the hill, and the lord paid him in gold coin to examine all his servants. By the time he had finished his rounds and was returning to the inn for dinner, most of the other villagers had gathered in the inn's common room, waiting to see him.

He was busy, but for the first time in a very long time, he was not unhappy. None of the villagers were in immediate danger of dying, and so he didn't see even the vision of Death for the next several days. The air was clear, the village beautiful, and he felt a strange sense of peace he'd never felt anywhere else.

On his third day in the village, he was eating his breakfast in the inn when a young woman approached him. Her hair was the color of dark wheat, loose around her face, and her eyes were round and gold, cat's eyes. She regarded him warily, hands clasped in front of her as if she might need to raise them quickly.

"Are you the doctor?" she asked. He nodded because his mouth was full of porridge. "My name is Hilda," she said. "If you would be willing, I have . . . a spot I'd like you to look at." Her face turned tomato red, and she cut her eyes toward the staircase and the front door, though no one had come in. "In return, I could mend any clothing you have, or if you'll be here for several more days, I could make you something new."

She was very pretty, he thought, and he disliked that she looked so uncomfortable with what she was asking. He swallowed and said, "Of course. If it requires privacy, I could visit you in your home."

Hilda nodded quickly. "Yes, thank you. I live in the cottage on the hill just behind the inn. Beneath the linden tree."

She hurried away, around the staircase and out of the inn, and he stared after her. He hadn't noticed a linden tree in the village.

After breakfast he had to make his first stop down by Grey

Lake. The fisherman, Falk, had a bad cough, and his wife was worried it was something worse, but still Death did not appear, and the doctor prescribed fluids and bed rest and as many fruits and vegetables as they could afford to trade for in the village. The whole while he was there, he was thinking of Hilda with her gold cat eyes and her discomfort. Was she in pain? Did she need his help urgently and she hadn't said so?

He hurried back to the village and went straight to the cottage behind the inn. It was there, on a hill, beneath a large and old linden tree, just as she'd said. He climbed the hill with long strides, but she had pulled the door open before he could reach the top.

"Thank you for coming," she said, welcoming him inside. The cottage was full of tailor's tools and a large loom. Hilda sat him down at the squat wooden table and closed the door behind him.

"If it was something urgent, I could have come sooner," he began.

She shook her head. "No, no, not urgent. I—I mean, it's not life-threatening, I just—oh, I *can't stand looking at it anymore!*"

She thrust out her hand. He realized then that she hadn't been holding her hands in front of her for protection; she'd been hiding one hand inside the other. Because there, on the knuckle of her left index finger, was a small, bulbous wart.

"Oh," he said.

"I *know* it's only a wart," she said, looking at the ceiling, "but I work with my hands all day and I see it there constantly and it's so—it's so—oh, I just don't like it!"

The doctor pressed his lips together to hold back his laughter. He normally didn't find humor in his patients' distress, but he was relieved it wasn't anything more serious, and she herself was smiling even as she cringed away from her own hand.

"I am very sorry this has caused you so much upset," he said, doing his best to keep his expression even, but seeing that sparkle of mirth in her eye and knowing she saw it in his, too, made it difficult. "I think I can help," he finally said. "Do you have vinegar?"

She brought him vinegar and water. He mixed the two, then had her sit with him at the table and he held her hand while he applied the mixture on the wart and bandaged it.

"Do this every night," he said, tying off the bandage, "and don't forget the water. Never put the vinegar on by itself; it'll burn you. The wart should fall off in about a week or so."

"Thank you," she said, relaxing a bit. "I feel very silly. I'm not usually so . . . excitable. I'm a very calm, dependable person."

"Is that so?"

"It is."

"Except with warts."

"Mmm. Warts, spiders, and children."

He frowned. "Warts and spiders I understand, but children?"

"I don't know what to do with them. I get nervous."

"Ah. Now that's a sentiment I can share."

She touched her hand, the bandage. Then she looked him once over. "The villagers have been calling you 'Doctor Death.' But that isn't your real name, of course."

"No. My name is Luther."

"Luther," she said. He liked the sound of it in her voice. He imagined she could make most things sound better just by being the one to say them. "How can I repay you?"

He wanted to say not to worry, that it hadn't exactly been a difficult diagnosis or remedy and he'd been happy to do it, but he was a consummate professional, and he didn't want her to take the gesture in a way that might make him seem otherwise.

"I'm afraid I don't travel with much in the way of clothing," he said, "but I have been meaning to purchase a new shirt. Something simple that won't wear out quickly. If it wouldn't be too much to ask."

"Not at all." She smiled. "I'll just need to take some measurements."

He stood in the middle of the small cottage while she measured his torso, shoulders, and arms. Hilda was by no means a small woman—she easily filled the cottage on her own—but the doctor had to duck to keep his head from hitting the beams. Hilda teased him about this, which he found he liked; people were usually too intimidated by him to tease him about anything. She touched him only lightly, fleeting brushes to prompt him to lift his arms, but even the lightest pressure seemed to leave a ghost imprint on his skin.

She told him she would have the shirt ready for him before he left town. That thought brought him down from the floating sense of contentment he'd felt since entering Greymist Fair, but he knew he had to go. He could feel Death growing impatient with his lingering, though he had stayed much longer in other places and Death had not minded. It didn't make sense to the doctor: the people of Greymist Fair died like the people anywhere else, and Death still took them, but Death either would not or could not visit the village willingly.

Hilda met him at the inn on the day he was to depart and presented him with the new shirt. It was a deep black and fit him perfectly.

"I prefer bright colors myself," she said, "but I thought you would appreciate black to go with all your black."

He had been more surprised and pleased with the shirt than he had expected, and he was so busy thanking her he almost missed it when she said, "If you like it so much, come visit me next time you pass through. I'll make you something else."

The invitation was enough to send him on his way. The sooner he left, the sooner he could return. He knew he would; Greymist Fair had become the magnetic north of his mind, and his internal compass would swivel toward it no matter where he went. The villagers bid him to return soon, and he assured them he would.

Death greeted him in the forest.

"That place will capture you and never let you go," said Death.

"That doesn't seem like such a poor fate," replied the doctor.

"I am not welcome there," said Death. "The villagers are cruel."

"They seemed lovely to me. Is that why you make the forest so dangerous for them? Because they don't welcome you? What makes them different from anyone else who fears you?"

"This is my home," Death said. "They are supposed to be my people."

"Perhaps if you approached them as a friend rather than an enemy, they wouldn't fear you so much."

Death looked away.

"I didn't know you could be so juvenile," said the doctor, and continued down the road.

He came back as he promised he would. The villagers warmly welcomed him and sought his care for their injuries and sicknesses. There were rarely any mortal illnesses when he visited, though when there were, Death appeared at the end of the bed, almost spiteful. It was the only time Death appeared in the village.

But those brief times of sadness never tainted the relief the doctor felt when he returned to Greymist Fair. He had never settled anywhere in his life, but sometimes when he was in the village, he found himself slipping into a routine that would mean settling if he continued it long enough. The villagers, though wary of him, wanted him there and appreciated his services, and he wanted to be there and to serve.

But each time he told himself that this was the *only* reason he came back, he was lying. His first thought was always of Hilda. After he arrived, got his room at the inn, and took care of any urgent medical issues, he went to see her. She would make tea and fill him in on the goings-on of the village, and he would tell her about his travels. A year and a half after his first visit, he knew where everything was in her cottage and was able to make the tea himself while she took a break from her work and watched him. He would help her with anything she needed, whether that was an aching tooth or a hole in her roof, and in return she made him a new article of clothing, always black. After three years, she'd made him a shirt, pants, gloves, boots, a coat, and—as a joke that had Hilda rolling on the floor with laughter at the expression on his face—a pair of black undergarments.

She'd meant them as a joke, but they were still wildly more comfortable than any he'd worn before.

They had islands of days in a sea of months when he was away traveling, and yet their time together stood out so brightly in his mind, it eclipsed the time they spent apart. They were not doctor and patient; they were friends and more than friends, although he didn't know how to broach that topic with her. How could he explain his relationship with Death to her? How could he be with anyone when Death was always there, calling Luther to their side?

None of that stopped him from thinking, each time he went away, about how he would feel if he returned to the village and discovered she had married. If she was happy, he would be happy for her, but he would also mourn for himself. What he had with her, he had with no one else. Not even Death.

Eight months had passed since Luther's last visit, and he had timed his return to coincide with the winter. He had never minded the winter; it was Death's season, and so it was his season. But it did make travel difficult, and he thought the weather might help him in his quest to stay longer than usual.

The village was preparing for the holiday festivities. The smaller evergreens from the edge of the forest had been cut and brought into homes to ward off darkness; evergreen garlands decorated eaves and windows, and evergreen wreaths hung from doors, fences, and the iron lampposts. Red bursts of holly and mistletoe highlighted doorframes and windowpanes. Handbells rang through the morning, and the smell of fresh gingerbread wafted from the bakery.

After settling in his room in the inn, the first thing the doctor did was ask after Hilda. She still lived in the cottage beneath the linden tree, and with some deft conversational maneuvering with the innkeepers, he found out she still lived there alone. He gathered a few bunches of holly with their bright red berries standing out against the snow, then a handful of snowdrops from around the side of the inn, where they grew in riots. He spent a moment arranging his little bouquet, then tied the red ribbon he'd brought from one of the great cities around the stems and finished it off with a bow.

He'd been practicing what he would say for months, and now, climbing the hill to her cottage, he disliked all of it. It all sounded rehearsed, wooden; he felt like a raggedy scarecrow with a bunch of weeds on his way to ask a beautiful maiden to consider him. Surely she had better prospects in the village. Someone good and respectable, who could settle with her and take care of her and who shared her understanding of the place they lived.

He could hear the clack of knitting needles and the crackle of fire on the other side of the door. She was in a good mood when she was knitting; knitting meant relaxing. The doctor breathed in, knocked three times, and waited. The clacking stopped. Soft footsteps approached the door. It swung open, letting out a puff of warm air.

There was a moment when her expression was open, blank, the moment before she recognized him. Watching the recognition hit her face was like watching the sun rise. Before he could say a word, her arms were around his neck, her body flush against his, the smell of dyes and wool heavy in his nose. They embraced tightly, teetering on the doorstep, until Hilda finally released him and took his face in her hands. Her smile was radiant. His hands settled on her waist, one still holding the bouquet.

"Where have you been?" she asked, straightening his hair with a flick of her fingers. "You were gone so long this time, I thought you weren't coming back."

His heart felt huge in his chest. He didn't think he could speak without choking. So much of his focus was going toward not holding her too tightly, not crushing her against him and never letting go. He handed her the bouquet.

"I come back for you," he said. "Always for you. You know that, don't you?"

She lifted her eyes from the bouquet and met his. "I had hoped so."

He was starving. For touch, for nearness, for warmth, for love. He wondered if she could see it in his face.

"Could we speak?" he asked. She stepped aside to let him into her cottage. She had changed nothing; she never did. The shutters were closed against the cold. She seemed to realize how hard he was trying to hold himself in place, because she only touched his sleeve lightly to urge him toward her little table. He didn't sit; he didn't think he could.

"You are the reason I come back here," he said again. "I love this village and the people in it, but it's you I think of when I'm gone, and it's you I want to see first when I return. I wonder if you're safe and happy. I wonder whether you found enough berries to make your favorite dye, or if your roof has started to leak again. I wonder if you have found someone who makes you happy. If you have decided to spend your life with them.

"But I have hesitated to tell you all of this. Not only because I didn't want to burden you with it, but because my life is not my own. I already share it with another, and this other can be . . . jealous."

She examined him closely, her eyes sharp, knowing. "Death," she said.

He wasn't surprised that she had guessed. It was in his name, after all. "Yes. Death is my parent, my sibling, my only friend. I am Death's companion. I am afraid what would happen if—"

"I am not afraid," Hilda said, resting her hand again on his cheek. Her palm was warm against his chilled skin. "I know Death, too. I visit Death often in the forest. I'm here to protect this village, so don't you worry about the people here, or about me. I may fear warts, and spiders, and children, but I do not fear Death."

The doctor was shaking, he wanted her so badly. "I can't always be with you. I wouldn't abandon my patients, and I must still spend time with Death. I can't promise how long I'll be gone. I can't provide for you or protect you the way another would. Despite all that, you would still have me?"

Smiling, she kissed him, and put her arms around him, and held him tight.

"I have never felt this way for anyone else," she said. "All the rest is detail."

four

They kept their relationship a secret. It would have been difficult if Hilda had not been able to wrap them both in her magic, one of the few times she ever used it for anything other than protecting the village. He didn't know how she did it, and he didn't ask. They did not lie to each other, but they did have secrets, and he thought this was good. He didn't need to know how she protected them; that was something she had learned from her mother, that her mother had learned from her grandmother, and on and on.

Every time he came back to Greymist Fair, the doctor rented his usual room in the inn, saw his patients, then went to Hilda. The time they spent together was consumed by touch, quiet conversations, the deepest, most restful sleep he had ever had, and the feeling that he was where he belonged. When he left, his memories of Hilda and her little cottage were cast in a golden light. On his travels, his most frequent thought was, *I cannot wait to go home.*

"I've never had a home before," he told Hilda the next winter, when they were twined together in her bed beneath furs he'd bought from Gottfried, and a fire crackled merrily in the hearth. "I have places I've been and places I'm going, but never a place of my own."

"Then this is yours," she said, kissing the end of his long and crooked nose. "Everyone deserves a home."

But the doctor could not go home as often as he liked; the more he visited Greymist Fair and the longer he disappeared into Hilda's cottage, the more withdrawn Death became. The doctor could sense Death's displeasure, but he didn't know that Hilda's magic was working against Death, too, until one summer afternoon while they walked together down a long and empty road, Death said to the doctor, "You have found something in that village. Someone else who will take you away from me."

"Of course not," said the doctor, flattening his hand nervously over the linden bloom inside his coat. "I only like it there because it's peaceful."

"Lots of villages are peaceful," said Death, but let the subject drop.

The doctor was wise enough by now to know that Hilda

could protect herself from Death, but it didn't stop him from worrying. The worry was small, though, and easily bested while he was traveling, while he could convince Death that there was no relationship in his life more important than the companion-ship they shared. It wasn't all lies; he did care for Death, and he understood Death's loneliness. He wanted to share with Death this love he had found, but he couldn't. Death would hate him for it. It was a burden he hadn't expected.

Then, after two years of secret keeping, the burden got heavier.

Luther returned from several months of travel, rented his room, and went to see his patients, and while he was examining one of the innkeepers, she said happily, "Have you been to see Hilda yet? You may not have heard, though it's been the talk of the village for the last month . . . No one knows who the father is—"

He didn't wait for her to finish. He was out of the inn, up the hill, and throwing the cottage door open before he could stop himself. Hilda jumped up from where she sat at her loom, threads in all shades of gold falling, and spun to face him. There was the pause, there was the dawning recognition, there was her smile.

She wore a loose dress, and her stomach swelled beneath it.

He cut his stay in the village short that time so that he could travel his rounds and be back in time for the birth. "You have to go," Hilda had told him when he insisted that he stay. "Death will get even more suspicious if you stay for that many months. Go now, and you'll be here when she's born."

So he left, his nerves frayed, and when he came back it was the height of summer. He waited outside the cottage while the midwife was inside with Hilda; the only reason he could even be there without raising suspicion was because he was Doctor Death, and he might be needed. He listened to Hilda's cries of pain and dug crescent moons into his palms with his nails. Suddenly he had a vision of entering the cottage and seeing Death standing at the end of Hilda's bed, black eyes blazing with the knowledge of their deceit, and both Hilda and the child lifeless in Death's shadow.

Another cry came through the open window. His daughter lived.

"Henrike," said Hilda, watching Luther hold the baby carefully along one forearm after the midwife had gone. "We'll call her Heike, for short."

"Little Heike," whispered the doctor. Little Heike slept, her round cheeks fuzzed like peaches and her eyelids almost trans-lucent. He could feel her mother's magic in her. "I have never seen anything so beautiful."

"Neither have I," said Hilda. But even as she smiled, lines of worry tightened around her eyes and mouth. Later, when the doctor forced himself to think of reality again, he knew what he had done to them. He could never truly be a father to his daughter, not while Death watched him so jealously. And she could never know who he was, lest she let slip the secret. It was too dangerous.

He lay in bed with Hilda, their bodies curved around Heike's small sleeping form, the room dark and the moon large in the sky outside the window.

"I told you once I didn't fear Death," she said, her voice hardly a whisper. "I realized it's not true anymore. I do fear Death. I fear *her* death. I fear mine, because if I'm not here, who will take care of her? Who will teach her about her magic, and what she needs to survive? I always thought my biggest fear would be not know-ing what to do with a child, how to take care of one, but this is so much bigger. I'm so afraid. I feel like I'll be afraid forever."

He found her hand in the darkness and brought it to his chest. "I will do everything in my power to keep her safe. To keep you both safe."

What he wanted to say was, *I'm afraid, too.* But he couldn't; to voice it was to admit it to himself. He could not allow himself to be afraid of Death. This was his duty, now. He had a home to protect, and he would protect it.

five

Luther could not be a father to Heike in the way she deserved, but he at least got to see her grow. And she grew quickly, as children do; he would leave and return and suddenly she was bigger, she was walking, she could speak. The mystery of the identity of her father lingered on in the village, but luckily, she had all her mother's features, except for her nose. Her nose was his, long and crooked.

Hilda kept a diary for him of Heike's days, when she spoke her first word, her first scraped knee, which foods she liked best. When Heike was still too young to remember him or understand what they were saying, he would sit with her in his lap in the cottage while Hilda read him the entries. Heike would grab at his fingers with her small pudgy hands. He would tell her how much he loved her, and as she grew closer to an age where there was a chance she would remember him, he would hug her close and cry.

He knew that time had come when Hilda sent Heike outside to play when he returned to Greymist Fair and showed up at the door.

"She asked me who her father is," Hilda said, peering out the window, where Heike was barreling down the hill to greet the little boy that had been adopted by the innkeepers. "I told her he's a good man, and he loves her very much."

"Does she believe you?" the doctor asked.

"I don't know." She turned away from the window to look at him. "Has Death noticed anything?"

"No. I made sure of that."

When the doctor was away from Greymist Fair, the energy not devoted to his patients was used convincing Death that there was nothing more important in the world to him than the bond they shared. Death, always so eager to banish loneliness, swallowed it whole. Gone was the withdrawal, the suspicion. Death was happy; Heike was safe.

Heike learned how to sew, like her mother. She wove magic into everything she made, though she didn't know it. She was good friends with the innkeepers' adopted boy, Wenzel, who asked Luther for stories of his travels. When Heike wasn't learning or doing chores, she was with Wenzel. He was one of the few people in town who would play with her.

Hilda's so-called involvement with the witch of the forest had caused the villagers to be wary of Heike as well. When her exclusion bothered him too much, he reminded himself how much worse it would be if people knew Doctor Death was her father. They valued his skills and his ability to help them, but they could sense what he was and where he came from.

When Heike was nine and Doctor Death came to the cottage to give her stitches, she regarded him with a new, thinly veiled distrust. With no preamble, she said, "Why do you look at my mother that way?"

It was a sharp question, demanding. She *was* a small Hilda, and his nose on her face couldn't do anything to dull the impression. "Look at her what way?" he asked, pretending not to understand.

Heike didn't seem to have words to answer him, because she screwed up her face and said, "You smell like . . . like winter, and dead things. You're not right, and you shouldn't look at her that way!"

"Henrike!" Hilda snapped, and the girl's temper fled in the presence of her mother's. "Apologize, now!"

"I won't." Heike wormed out of her chair, slipped around the doctor, and ran to the door. "I don't like him, and I don't want him here."

He thought she would run out then and console herself outdoors, but she pushed open the door and stood by it, staring at him, waiting. Her anger had been quelled, but not her sense of duty.

"*Henrike!*" Hilda's tone was dangerous, but Heike didn't move.

"I'll go," said the doctor quietly, and he looked at neither Hilda's face nor Heike's as he gathered his things and left.

Hilda found him at the inn later and apologized—"She just doesn't know . . . she's so protective . . . she thinks someone will take me away from her"—but she didn't have to. The doctor had spent enough time with jealous Death to understand. And now that Heike was getting older, loving her mother as much as she did, their world was closing its doors to him. His sun-dappled memories of the years he'd spent with Hilda in the home they'd made together began to fade.

When he left Greymist Fair after that visit, Death was in high spirits.

Death could be in many places at once, as was the nature of their being, but the doctor noticed their absence the moment he entered the forest heading toward Greymist Fair, and he did not see Death until a week later, when he had left the village again and exited the forest on the far side. Heike was four-teen now, a gangly girl who was already taller than her mother, and she kept a good distance between herself and the doctor, though Hilda said she had forgotten her dislike for him. It made him feel even more out of sorts, and he had felt like that often these days.

"You must be careful." Death appeared at the doctor's side, gliding along on the shadows cast by the blue-flame lanterns. "There is a witch in that village, and if she learns of your relation to me, she will kill you."

"Witch?" the doctor said, trying to keep his face emotion-less.

"The tailor," said Death. "She visits my home in the forest to ensnare me, to keep me from entering the village in person. She thinks I should be alone, that I should have no companionship. She thinks I am not worthy of it."

"You do kill the people who enter the forest," the doctor pointed out.

"Only because they fear me!" Death's placid expression twisted in fury. Needle teeth flashed against thin, pallid lips. Black eyes became empty pits. "If they did not fear me, I would have companionship, and none would have to die save for illness, injury, and age. I would not have to twist the wargs to my service. It is her fault, the witch! She poisons the town with her fear! But I see it in her . . . I've seen that same fear. I've seen that daughter of hers. When she came to see me this time, I knew she feared me, but I couldn't catch her."

The doctor's heart pounded in his chest. He had to remind himself that he had just seen Hilda in the village; she was alive and well. "What do you mean? She outran you?"

"She put magic in her boots," Death said. "And she ran for home. Only that allowed her to escape from me. But I am waiting for her, and it's only a matter of time. You must be careful in the village. Don't let her know who you are. She will kill you."

The doctor clenched his hand at his side to stop himself from putting it over his heart, where he always kept the sprig of linden in his inner pocket. Being apart from Hilda was bad enough; knowing she had been in such danger, that she could be in danger again, was worse.

Death continued to complain about the witch of Greymist Fair, and the doctor allowed it. For while Death was angry about her, Hilda was still alive.

I am waiting for her, and it's only a matter of time.

The time was two years. The doctor had been away from Greymist Fair for almost ten months, one of his longer trips, and he returned to news that made the world slide away from him.

Two of the village children, the butcher's boy and Lord Greymist's own daughter, had gone into the forest to find the witch. Hilda had followed to stop them. The boy had gotten out—that one was too self-important to fear Death, the doctor thought—but the girl, Katrina, had been killed by the wargs. Lady Greymist, distraught, had taken ill and not recovered. Now the once hale and hearty Lord Greymist was dying as well, and the village was in mourning.

Katrina had left no remains save her shoes and some scraps of her dress. That was the fate of all innocents who died in the forest and in Greymist Fair; they became wargs themselves.

So they assumed that was also what had happened to Hilda.

Delirious, the world shrinking around him, the doctor managed to ask only one question. He directed it at Wenzel, who had recounted the story, and who had taken over the inn after the old innkeepers passed away.

"The shoes they found," the doctor said, "were they her boots, the ones with the long laces and the ribbons she liked to wind through them?"

"Oh no," said Wenzel. "She was wearing an older pair while

she made a second set for herself. She gave the ones with the ribbons to Heike."

Of course you did, the doctor thought. He kept thinking it as he went up to his room, put his face in his hands, and began laughing and crying at the same time.

Of course you did, and now Heike has no one, because you are gone and I can never claim her.

Death never said a thing about finally besting the witch of Greymist Fair. The doctor wondered if it hadn't been as sweet a victory as Death had hoped after all.

six

Doctor Death stayed away from the village for a long time after that, figuring Heike would be safer if he returned only rarely and did not interact with her. He suffered bouts of fancy now and then, thinking that if he wandered into the forest he might be able to find Hilda. He knew he would love her spirit even in the body of a warg. But it was all make-believe. When he returned to reality, he carried on with his business. He saw his patients; he saw Death at the foot of many beds; he did what he could and helped where he was able.

When he finally returned to Greymist Fair again, he had forgotten how many years had passed. It was late fall, the cusp of winter. Wenzel was a fine young man, happy and welcoming, and he remembered what the doctor liked for breakfast and how he took his tea, and he still asked for stories from afar. He was writing a storybook, he said.

As the doctor was sitting down for his toast and jam, the

door opened, and Heike came in. She looked so much like Hilda that for a moment the doctor's heart was wrenched from his chest in disbelief, and he nearly shoved himself up from the table and called her name. Then his mind caught up to him. His daughter—*his* daughter, it was strange to call her that now, because she seemed so much her own woman, and he had played so little a role in her upbringing—was standing by the stairs with an empty berry basket and flirting with Wenzel about strange things happening across the Idle River Bridge.

She left again without so much as a glance his way. That was as it should be, but his appetite was gone.

When she returned later that day with a report of a murder on the road—not in the forest, but *on the road*—he knew that something had stirred Death. The villagers thought it was the witch, but the villagers also thought the witch controlled the wargs. He could not tell them the truth, nor could he tell Heike the truth when she volunteered to go into the forest. Not because he thought telling her the truth would put her in any greater danger than walking right up to Death's doorstep, but because he didn't want to. She had her mother's training; she had her mother's boots. He didn't blame her for her mother's death—he was no longer so depraved as that—but he didn't think there was anything he could say or do that would stop her.

She had her mother's sense of duty as well.

He did catch her before she left, though. He met Heike, Wenzel, and Ulrich behind the inn, and Heike watched him with those wary gold eyes.

"Head northwest," he told her, remembering what Hilda had once told him of her excursions into the forest. "If you reach the bend of the Idle River, you've gone too far."

"You know where the house is?" Heike asked.

Hearing her speak directly to him was a brush of warmth on his long-numbed heart, and he found it difficult to reply. He reached into one of his pockets and pulled out a small leather pouch he kept packed with sage. He removed a dried bunch and gave it to her.

"Keep this with you. In a pocket where it won't fall out. Not in your bag. You might lose that."

It wouldn't invoke Death's wrath if it was found, but it might offer her some protection.

She tucked it away and said, "Thank you."

"Safe journey," he said, hearing his voice shake, feeling his whole body shake. He swallowed thickly and said, "Your mother prepared you well."

For the rest of the afternoon and evening, he sat in his room and worried, thinking of all the ways he could better help Heike, all the things he could be doing for her, all the things he could have told her. For much of that time, he thought, *You should have told her, you coward.* And the rest of the time, he thought, *You can't protect her forever.*

The doctor didn't stop worrying even after she came back. He didn't stop worrying when Jürgen the butcher turned up dead in the well, and a ragged batch of children was freed from beneath his house. The doctor didn't stop worrying when elk stampeded through the village, when the weather turned for the worse, or when, without warning, Jürgen's son, Hans, was suddenly the king, and a castle had grown out of Greymist Manor. None of the villagers seemed to realize that this reality had not always been their reality, and it was over only a few hours after it began, like a very strange dream.

It was not a dream when Heike was brought to the inn. He had carried her up to a room, and as soon as she was put on the bed, he made everyone—the fisherman's boy and his friend, Wenzel, and Ulrich—get out. Because Death was standing at the end of the bed, looking down on Heike.

She *was* dying, and the doctor guessed it had something to do with the magic that had been required to strip the boy king of his power and return the village to normal. He could see the color draining from her face, like an oil lamp inside her was being slowly turned down. Her light would be snuffed out, and soon.

He looked at her. He looked at Death. No medical treatment would bring her back now. No amount of wishes or prayers. He knew this. He had been through it enough times with others. But Heike wasn't *others*, and all those places he'd been weren't his home.

He reached into his coat pocket, the one over his heart, and drew out the sprig of linden blooms, as fresh and yellow as the day they had been tucked into his swaddling blanket. Death's gaze was drawn to them.

"What are you doing?" Death asked.

The doctor placed the linden bloom over Heike's heart and folded her hands atop it. Right away, the blue tips of her fingers turned pink again. Color filled her cheeks. Her breathing slowed and evened.

Death stared at the doctor, incredulous. "You choose her over me? What has she given you that I haven't?"

"It isn't you or her," said the doctor. "You've never understood. People fear you because you force them to choose you at the exclusion of all others. If you continue that way, you will always be alone. I love you and what you have done for me, but I have loved others, too, and my love for them did not diminish my love for you. It only hindered it, because I couldn't share them with you, or you with them."

"But . . . how could you love her? She's the witch's daughter. The witch who kept me from my home . . ." Death looked betrayed.

"Her name was Hilda. You would have terrorized this village if she hadn't protected them from you. Neither she nor her daughter deserved your wrath."

Death paused, dark eyes scanning the doctor's face. "You loved her."

"Yes."

"And this girl . . ." Death looked down at Heike.

"She's my daughter."

The doctor had known giving Heike the linden sprig was the last thing he would ever do. He would never have parted with it for anyone else, except Hilda.

Death appeared before the doctor, and when the doctor looked down, he saw Death's arm buried in his chest, and he felt Death's hand locked around his heart. Death was crying. The doctor felt only a strange sensation of floating.

Then he left the inn and returned to sunlit days beneath a linden tree, with Hilda's fingers in his hair, the breeze soft on his skin, and a sense that time, for just a little while, had stopped.

THE WARGS
OF GREYMIST

one

A chorus of screams rose from the forest surrounding Greymist Fair.

Wenzel, pacing the room, lurched for the window, ignoring the flash of pain across his back. There was only darkness outside the inn, but he could sense something out there rushing into the village, the screams becoming howls, like wolves. The windows rattled. Then the moment passed, and Wenzel stood, hairs raised and heart beating erratically, knowing something terrible had just happened.

He burst out of his room and pushed his way into Heike's before Fritz, his friend Altan, or Ulrich could stop him. Heike was in bed, her hands closed over her heart, and Doctor Death was slumped against the far wall. Wenzel kneeled next to him. He was cold and still, his eyes open but unseeing.

"He's dead?" Altan asked. "But how? We were standing right outside."

Wenzel pulled himself up to the bedside. Heike's chest rose and fell with her breathing, and her cheeks were a healthy pink. Her hands were folded over a linden bloom.

Outside, the enraged screams of the wargs echoed in the night.

Heike's eyes opened slowly. She looked around at all of them, at Doctor Death, up at Wenzel. "What happened?"

"The doctor saved you," Ulrich said. Then, to Fritz and Altan, he said, "Help me move him. He's not from Greymist Fair. The forest won't take him—"

But even as he spoke, the doctor's body vanished in a slice of shadow, leaving only the tatters of his black coat and his shoes behind. They all stood very still, as if a warg might materialize in the room and claim every one of them. A breathless second passed. Another. None of them had ever seen someone become a warg. Very carefully, Fritz picked up the shreds of clothing and the shoes and took them from the room. Altan, looking stunned, followed.

Heike was trying to sit up in bed, but her arms were shaking. Wenzel helped her and stuffed pillows against the headboard so she'd be comfortable. "Is everything back to the way it should be?" Heike asked. She frowned at the impossible linden bloom in her hand but didn't let go of it. "Is Hans . . . ?"

"Driven into the forest," Wenzel said. "But something new has happened. I don't know if it was caused by the magic, or by Hans, or by something else entirely. The wargs—" Screams and howls filled the air once again, driving chills up Wenzel's arms. "They're here. I think they're all here."

"The wargs belong to Death," Heike said, leaning her head back and closing her eyes, her brow furrowed. "If the wargs are angry, Death is angry. But it's been weeks since I went to the cottage in the woods. Why would . . ." She opened her eyes, looked down at the linden bloom. "I was dying, wasn't I?"

Wenzel couldn't bring himself to confirm it, but Ulrich nodded. Heike glanced at the spot where Doctor Death had slumped against the wall. "I was supposed to die, but he saved me. Death wanted me dead very badly when we spoke in the forest. I imagine having that satisfaction taken away would be frustrating."

"Death can hang," said Ulrich. "Most of the village is crammed in downstairs. I'll go see what we can find out about what's happening outside."

After he left, Heike took Wenzel's hand. "Your back. I thought reversing the wish would heal it."

Wenzel shrugged. "It wasn't a deep cut. I'll be fine. I'm only glad we don't live in that awful world anymore. Don't worry about me, though—you're in worse shape. I should get you something to eat. And you should try to sleep."

She held his hand tightly. "I won't be able to sleep while Death has decided to attack the village. Stay with me. We should be safe so long as we aren't afraid, and it's much easier to be brave when you're here." She smiled weakly. "Tell me some stories. Or better yet, finish writing them down. Make me that storybook you promised me."

Wenzel lifted her hand and kissed her fingers, then rubbed them between his own to warm them. "I don't know if now is the time for stories," he said. "Besides, I'm not much of a writer."

"You're an excellent writer," she replied, but let the subject drop.

They sat together and listened to the murmur of voices downstairs, and the occasional howls outside. Eventually Fritz shouldered his way back into the room with a tray of hot stew. He set it across Heike's legs.

"Gabi said you should eat and then come downstairs, if you feel strong enough," Fritz said. "There's a meeting to decide what should be done about the wargs."

The few brave enough to go outside—Gottfried the hunter and his husband, Oswald, Dagny the baker, Ulrich, and Elma Klein—hadn't been able to see the wargs in the darkness, and there had been no tracks in the snow, but there were traces of destruction. Yule garlands had been torn from fences and eaves, wreaths swiped down from doorways by great claws that left gouges in the doors, and animals sheltered from the cold in barns kicked and butted at their stalls in fear. Gottfried felt hunted but couldn't see his stalker.

"It was Dagny who saw Death." Fritz's voice was quiet. "On the rise by Greymist Manor, silhouetted in a shaft of moonlight. They're thinking of sending out a hunting party to find Death and . . . well, and kill them, though I don't know how they plan to do that."

"They can't." Heike sat forward, jostling the tray and the stew bowls. "You can't fight Death with guns and axes. Wenzel, help me up—we have to get downstairs."

Wenzel took the tray, and he and Fritz helped Heike from bed. She teetered on her feet, had to pause to get her bearings, and then had to lean on Wenzel as they shuffled out the door and down the stairs.

The conversation in the inn common room had risen to shouting. Fritz helped wedge a path through the villagers, and Wenzel held Heike close to his side so she wouldn't be jostled by the crowd. At the far end of the room, by the fireplace, Ulrich, Godric, and Elma stood arguing about their hunting plans, each backed by their own supporters. The yelling made Wenzel's muscles instinctively tighten, even after all these years, so he had to be careful not to hold Heike too hard.

When Heike came into view, the villagers fell quiet. The apothecary jumped up from his chair and offered it to her. Heike sank into it with a breathless "Thank you."

"This isn't going to work," she said in the silence. "You all know it. It doesn't matter what time of day you go out, or how many weapons you take, or what kind of traps you try to set. Death can't be killed, only temporarily staved off."

"Then what do you suggest we do?" Godric the blacksmith asked. "Stay here until the food runs out? Until the firewood is gone and the cold takes us? We can't leave or the wargs will kill us."

"The wargs shouldn't be like this. In the old stories, they were guides. Helpers. Not killers. They attack because we're afraid. Only while we fear Death are we in danger. We have to banish this fear, and the village will be safe again."

"How?"

"We celebrate Yule."

The howl of wargs cut through the sudden silence.

"*Celebrate?*" someone called from behind Wenzel. "We're supposed to *celebrate* while Death is tearing at the doors?"

"We'll let our guards down and the wargs will get in!" someone else said.

"And the village gifts," cried a small voice from the edge of the room. "The gifts will be left on the edge of the forest."

Wenzel turned, looking for the child in a sea of clamoring adults. The village gifts were a donation from an unseen friend, and they appeared each year at the far edge of the forest, where the road left the protection of the trees and continued into the world beyond. Small toys for the children and wrapped parcels of meat, bread, pies, and other foods for the annual village feast. The innkeepers had once been the ones to fetch the gifts. The feast was held in the inn common room and lasted for several days and nights. Since the innkeepers had passed on, the responsibility had fallen to Wenzel. The gifts would be waiting.

"I can go," he said, though no one seemed to hear him except for Heike. She spun in her chair so quickly she groaned and had to hold her head. "I'll go to the edge of the forest to retrieve the village gifts," he repeated.

This time others heard him, and the room quieted once again. Frowns crossed faces. Some began to protest. Ulrich stepped toward him. "Wenzel, the gifts can be set aside for now. They aren't important. You can't risk yourself on the road."

Wenzel gripped the back of Heike's chair. "They *are* important.

The feast is important. We celebrate a new year, and hope it brings us good fortune and prosperity. We remember what brings us all together. Are any of us thinking of a future right now? Are any of us looking at one another and remembering what binds us? We're all gathered here. We're together, not alone. Wouldn't you rather see the children playing? Wouldn't you rather have roast boar and hot pies to fill your stomach?"

Mutters rose. Ulrich glanced at Gabi, who had her palm to her forehead. The tension in the room had been reduced to a low simmer, tinged with new questions.

A hand settled on Wenzel's. Heike looked up at him. "You're too important. I can go."

Wenzel laughed. "*I'm* too important? Heike, you're . . . I'm just an innkeeper. And it's my duty, anyway. And besides all that, you almost died. You can't even turn in your chair without getting dizzy." She looked like she wanted to argue more, but her face was turning green, and she clamped her mouth shut. Wenzel raised his voice and spoke to the room. "I'll go by horse. I believe Heike that Death won't be able to take me as long as I'm not afraid." And before they could ask how he would defeat fear, before they could guess whether he had even a *shred* of doubt inside him, he smiled and said, "I'll think of all of you."

two

Wenzel had always been afraid. When he was very young, in those earliest memories that surfaced in his conscious mind only rarely these days, he had been afraid of his father, and raised voices, and the leather sting across his back. He had been afraid of darkness, the calls of mourning doves, and the looks of exasperation and annoyance he got whenever he began to cry. He became afraid of crying.

But as he dressed and gathered what he needed to journey out on the road, he fought fear off with the thought of things that made him happy. New stories for his collection. The crackling of the fire in the inn's common room. The excited squeals of children chasing each other across the village square on fine-weather days. The contentment on Heike's face when he brought her a warm bowl or mug to wrap her cold fingers around. He was going on this journey to save those things. That would keep him brave. And when he returned, he'd have his own story to tell.

Gabi checked and rewrapped Wenzel's bandages before he put on his shirt. The cuts weren't deep, but he wasn't looking forward to the pain he'd have if he burst Doctor Death's stitches. He thought of the tall doctor, slumped against the wall. Disappearing. He wondered if the doctor was out in the forest now.

"You should be able to lift the sack of gifts onto the horse," Gabi said, "but anything more strenuous than that and you'll open yourself up again."

He didn't plan on doing anything more strenuous. It had always been a simple task, and he would think of it as that now. A nice ride down the road, the pickup, and the ride home.

Heike sat on the edge of his bed, looking peaky, while he dressed. She twirled the linden bloom between her fingers. "Not that one," she said as he pulled a rough work shirt from the tall wooden armoire. "The one I made you last week."

"But you just made it," he said. "It's so nice."

"Wear it," she said. "It's for a reason."

He returned the shirt and pulled out the other. Plain, bleached white, and still soft. He pulled it on over his head and immediately felt a little warmer. He finished dressing—coat, scarf, gloves, hat—and when he finally turned back to Heike, he found her, grabbing her boots from the floor.

"You need to take these, too," she said.

"I think my feet are too big."

She gave him a withering look and began tying the ends of the laces together. She motioned him closer and tugged his sleeve to get him to bend down, and then she looped the laces over his neck so the boots hung against his chest. "I know it's strange. Just take them." Then, before he could rise, she took hold of his scarf where it was knotted beneath his chin. Exhaustion hung under her eyes, but her gaze was intent, and her voice was strong. "I want you to do this, and I want you to return, and I want you to remember that when you desired to do something noble for Greymist Fair, I did not try to stop you."

She didn't let go of his scarf. The knuckle of her thumb was cold on his chin. He nodded and said softly, "I'm sorry, Heike. I was selfish."

She pulled him closer and kissed his cheek, sending a chill down his neck. "I know why you did it, though," she said. "If you get into any trouble, run straight ahead and think of home."

Firelight, bright smiles, contentment, and warmth. This was what he thought of as he saddled his horse and set out. He had consented to waiting until the sun was rising, so at least the daylight—even if the sun was hidden behind clouds—would help ease any fear. The horses had calmed, too, as had the villagers in the inn. The village itself had settled into stillness. Wenzel did not look up at Greymist Manor as he passed through the town square and headed for the road into the forest.

Warm mugs. Spring berries. The roses blooming on the face of the inn.

He had first made this journey when he was only seven or eight. He had wanted to go so badly, but had known better than to ask, and the innkeepers—his adoptive mother and father—had finally relented. His father had taken him along for the ride and taught him why it was such an important duty. He hadn't really needed to be told, though. He already knew why it was important to bring Yule to the village. Everyone needed a place and reason to celebrate, and people to celebrate with.

Before they had adopted him, he had only seen holidays from afar, either the holidays celebrated by traveling caravans or by the people in the villages and towns the caravans visited. His father—rather, the man who had been responsible for him—had never celebrated anything.

Johanna, the baker, had once asked Wenzel why he never seemed angry or unhappy. "Because there's nothing so bad here to be angry or unhappy about," he'd told her with a smile. It was the truth, but only part of it; he couldn't bring himself to be angry or unhappy about anything that happened to him in Greymist Fair, because if he hadn't been abandoned there, his life probably would have been miserable. If he'd had a life at all. His parents had saved him. The village had given him purpose. He was happy the day he chose a new name for himself, a name that had never been screamed at him, and he was happy every day he got to use it.

He hunkered into his scarf and coat. Heike's boots rocked rhythmically against his chest. The road was obscured by snow, only visible because of the lampposts poking out of the drifts like crooked iron fingers. He told himself the road was as always: winding but safe. He told himself he didn't feel the eyes of the forest following him, its fingers trailing over his neck and shoulders, through his hair. Every so often he glanced sideways into the trees, pretending that he was just curious and didn't care if he saw a warg there.

There was nothing. He wondered how such a thick layer of snow had found its way down between the boughs of the evergreens.

What most people disliked about the road was that it always seemed to take a different amount of time to traverse it. Wenzel had never noticed this. He spent the time thinking about projects around the inn he had completed and what still needed to be done. He thought about things his neighbors had done for him, and how they could be repaid. He went through his mental catalogue of stories he'd collected from people who had visited Greymist Fair. In his mind, the world beyond the forest was huge and beautiful, with towering cities and sweeping oceans, mountain ranges that pierced the sky and opened gateways to the gods, magic that was even wilder and stranger than the magic that lived in Greymist Fair. Heike had long encouraged him to write these stories down, to make a book of them, and not so long ago he'd been sweeping the inn's front walk, thinking he should do just that. He'd jotted down a few, but a whole book? Who would care about a book of his stories?

His horse huffed as it clattered over the Idle River Bridge. The river beneath, normally powerful and relentless even in the winter, was frozen solid. Wenzel noted this and looked away.

The singing of orioles. Cold, clear water on a hot summer day. The feeling of being clean after a long time being dirty.

He hadn't even realized how dirty he was until his parents had taken him in. Sometimes one of the caravan members would dunk him in a river or stream when they said he smelled too bad, but he'd never had a proper bath until he was found on Elma Klein's farm. The water had been cold, the soap rough on his skin, and he'd cried when they'd cut his matted hair off, but when it was over, he was dressed in a clean nightshirt and plopped in front of the fire with a meat pie and mead. He'd devoured the meat pie and chased it with mead, which he hadn't recognized until he was almost done. He lasted only a short time after that. He slept for a whole day and woke up in a bed much bigger than him.

His life before waking up in that bed now seemed like a nightmare he'd had as a child, vividly real but at the same time nothing that could hurt him any longer. He didn't want to be that scared little boy again.

When he reached the far edge of the forest, the trees dropped away suddenly, as if they had hit an invisible barrier they couldn't cross. Foothills rolled away into the foggy distance. There was not another living soul as far as he could see, neither animal nor human, and the effect was what he imagined being a ghost might feel like. This was his favorite part of the trip, always. Standing on the edge of the forest, looking out into a world unknown.

Standing here, it seemed that the terror that gripped Greymist Fair was a world away. No one beyond the borders of their forest knew what was happening in the village. No one knew their fear, and no one would come to help them. There was only Wenzel.

The clouds cracked and parted; the sun was already high

above, though Wenzel hadn't felt like he'd been traveling all that long. Even his legs and back didn't protest when he swung himself off his horse. He stretched a bit, testing his bandages, but all seemed well.

He began to hunt for the sack of gifts. It was the same every year: a tough, green-dyed sack nearly as big as Wenzel, tucked into the curling roots of a massive old oak that stood to one side of the road. The sack would be invisible to anyone who wasn't expecting it to be there. No one in the village knew who left it, or when they had started riding down the road to retrieve it, but it came every year and every year they accepted it.

He tromped along the line of trees to the old oak. The snow covered everything, so at first he didn't think much of not seeing the sack. But it was over half his size, and if there was anything buried beneath the snow at the foot of the oak, it wasn't very big. In fact, as he drew closer, there was a noticeable disturbance in the snow. There had been something large sitting there, but now there was only a pit. And there were other footprints leading around the trees from inside the forest.

Wenzel tensed. The prints were his size. Booted. Fresh.

A voice spoke behind him.

"I was waiting, Grub."

three

Hans held the handles of the green-dyed sack in swollen red fingers. He watched Wenzel with dark, exhausted eyes. Frostbite had set in on his nose, ears, and lips. The right side of his face blistered where Heike had hit him with the bed warmer. He wore the clothes he had been wearing when the villagers had chased him from his castle, though his golden crown was gone. In his free hand he held one of his father's long carving knives.

"Let's go, Grub," he said. "You're helping me get back to the village."

"Helping you?" Wenzel replied. "You can get there yourself. Follow the road. But I can't promise you'll be welcomed when you arrive." The villagers still remembered what Hans had done to them; they would leave him outside for Death and the wargs.

"That's what you're for." Hans flicked the knife toward the horse and the road. "We're going to say that you nearly died trying to get the village gifts, and I saved you and brought you back.

They'll see that I've repented, and they'll welcome me."

"Why do you want to return? There's nothing there for you. Go somewhere else." Wenzel extended an arm to the misty foothills. "Go *anywhere*."

Hans bared his teeth. "Greymist Fair is my home."

"You would return to a home that doesn't want you?"

"It's the only one I have."

Hans's grip didn't look especially tight on the knife, and if he had frostbite, he was probably close to hypothermia as well. Wenzel suspected he would be faster and stronger than Hans even with the wound in his back, so he wasn't particularly worried about getting hurt, but there was something to be said for desperation.

And you aren't going to leave him out here to die, he thought to himself. He'd never liked Hans—downright hated him, especially after his brief stint as king—but he didn't think he could live with himself if he knew he had left someone to die. He'd always felt bad for Hans; Hans had never escaped his cruel father the way Wenzel had. But that wasn't an excuse for the things he'd done since.

"Bring the sack," Wenzel said. "If you can't lift it, leave it there and I'll get it."

Hans must have lifted and dragged it to get it where he

stood, but he released the rope handle and stepped back, holding the knife aloft. The sack weighed a good amount, though it never seemed heavy enough for all the food and toys they pulled from it. Careful of his back, Wenzel hefted the sack over his shoulder and carried it to the horse, where he secured it on the saddle.

"Out of the way," Hans said. "I've been walking through this damned forest all night. I want to ride. And then you can't run off with the gifts and leave me." He shoved his boot into a stirrup and tried to lift himself up, but his desperate bout of energy seemed to have fled. With a sigh, Wenzel dropped down, grabbed Hans's foot, and boosted him into the saddle. Hans glared at Wenzel and settled himself. The horse flicked its ears back in annoyance.

"Don't ride off without me," Wenzel said. "You need me to corroborate your story. You try telling them I died out here but you managed to save the gifts, they'll know you're lying."

Hans peered down his nose. "Give me your coat, Grub. It looks warm."

"You survived in the forest all night in your own clothes, you'll last a while longer."

Hans jabbed Wenzel's shoulder with the knife. "Hey!" Wenzel jumped away from the horse. Maybe he'd been wrong about being faster.

"*Coat,*" Hans sneered.

Wenzel unfastened his coat and tossed it up to Hans, resettling Heike's boots on his chest. He'd expected the cold to cut through the thin shirt, but he felt just as warm as he had before. Hans slid the coat on, all the while looking down at Wenzel with annoyance. "Why're you wearing boots around your neck?"

"Extra pair in case some ass with a knife takes mine," Wenzel said.

Hans's lip curled.

They took the road in silence. Heike had said fear of Death brought the wargs, so the only way Hans could have survived a night in the forest was if he wasn't afraid of Death. What had fueled him, then? Anger? The desire to return to a village that had thrown him to the trees? Wenzel glanced up at Hans and saw in profile that empty expression that Hans wore so often, as if he were vacant on the inside, a house with no human occupants. Hans's hands were hidden inside Wenzel's coat now, but Wenzel no longer expected him to be clumsy or slow. That knife could come flashing out again in an instant.

"I don't understand," Hans said when they reached the Idle River Bridge, "why they all like you so much. You aren't even *from* Greymist Fair."

Wenzel made sure he was a little more than arm's length

from the horse before he said, "Perhaps it's because I don't try to enslave them to carry out my every whim."

Hans didn't seem to hear him. "There's nothing special about you. You're not particularly good at anything, you don't have money, you're not funny or attractive—"

"I think that's subjective—"

"—and *you're not from here*. You don't even *belong*. So why do they like you more than me? Why have they always liked you more than me?"

Wenzel rolled his eyes. "I don't know, Hans. Because I'm *kind* to people? Because I don't berate them, or use them? How do you not understand this? Are you that unobservant?"

"Is Fritz still in the village?" Hans asked. "Did they kick him out, too?"

"Fine, ignore me. Don't try to grow as a person."

"Answer me, Grub."

"Shut up."

The knife flashed. Wenzel jerked out of the way just in time, but his cheek stung, and when he put his glove to it, his fingertips came away splotched with blood.

"Will you *stop* that?" Wenzel snapped. "There are *real* problems in the village right now because of you, and I'm trying to fix them. I don't have time for your pettiness!"

"Oh, *real* problems? I'm sure there are." Hans's lip curled. "Not enough garlands for *every* fence row? No one found a good Yule log?"

"No. Death attacked the village with his wargs."

Quickly, Wenzel went back to his list of things that made him happy. Fresh milk with the cream gathered on top. The inn's front walk right after he swept it. The smell of cut wood.

"Death attacked?" Hans said, looking down in surprise. "And you coming out here was to help? How do you know anyone there is still alive?"

Wenzel shivered. He didn't know; he hadn't thought about that. It was well past midday and might be dark by the time they reached the village. Something could have happened in that time. He might return to a village of wargs.

"I believe they're all okay," he said aloud, to reassure himself.

Hans scoffed. "*Believe* all you want; the wargs are vicious. They'll tear everyone apart. That's what they did to Katrina. You remember that, don't you? That's what they did to Hilda, too. They tear them apart to kill them. And later their corpses become wargs."

"Shut *up*, Hans."

Hans smiled. "Making you nervous? If the wargs can come into the village now, I doubt anything will stop them from jumping through the windows. They'll go for the children first, probably. The smallest and weakest. Or maybe they'll gang up on the biggest and strongest first, so they can have their way with the others."

Wenzel felt his pulse in his ears. Shadows appeared on the edge of his vision. The horse's ears flicked back and forth, its eyes rolling. "Hans, you need to stop—"

Hans was smiling down at him now, the empty smile of an animal toying with its prey. "They'll get to Heike, too, all alone in her little cottage on the hill. What part do you think they'll tear open first? Her chest or her face?"

Heike will be okay, Wenzel thought. *Heike will be okay, Heike will be okay, Heike will be okay.*

But what if she wasn't?

A shadow darted across the road. The horse screamed and reared back and sideways, throwing Wenzel off his feet. He landed on his back with a bolt of pain. The horse's hooves tossed snow over him as it took off—not down the road, but into the forest—with Hans and the sack of gifts on its back.

four

"N**o**!"

Wenzel lurched to his feet and took off after the horse. Heike's boots banged against his chest. Hans's voice echoed through the trees as he yelled at it to stop, but nothing was going to stop the horse now for low, four-legged shadows pursued them. They were perfectly black against the blinding white snow, with no definitions to their features. It was as if pieces of the world had been cut out, and all that was left were the fathoms of beyond.

But Wenzel quickly realized that while the horse was running from the wargs, the wargs weren't pursuing the horse. The wargs had never killed animals. They were pursuing *Hans. He* was the one that was afraid.

Baking bread. The satisfaction of repairing one of the common room chairs or tables. Getting a new spice from the caravan traders.

"Hans!" he called. "Hans, grab the reins—"

The horse had disappeared between the trees, and when he saw it again, some way in the distance, neither Hans nor the sack of gifts was on its back anymore. Wenzel kept running—he dared not do anything else—and charged through between trees to where he thought Hans must have fallen.

Something heavy slammed into his back, throwing him forward into the snow. Hands turned him over, and a weight dropped onto his chest, making it hard to breathe. He blinked the snow out of his eyes.

Hans sat on him, burnt and frostbitten face twisted, knife held to Wenzel's throat.

"You scared the horse," Hans seethed. "You're trying to get me lost in the woods again. Trying to kill me."

Wenzel could see the wargs on the edges of his vision, lurking behind the trees. "No—no, I was trying to *help* you."

"Stop lying," Hans said. "I know you all hate me. Heike hates me. The adults hate me. Liesel hated me." His lips twisted. "It was easy to push her. You all hate me so much, you'd have thrown me out like you did from the castle. You'd kill me the moment you get the chance."

"I wouldn't."

"I said *stop lying*." The knife pressed against Wenzel's throat. "I know you would. They all would. You think I don't know people hate me? They think I'm *wrong,* that I'm cruel. Just like my father, they say. Maybe they won't let me back in if you're dead, but I won't get back at all if you're alive, will I? You'll kill me before I get the chance."

"Why do you want to go back so badly? Why not go somewhere that people don't know who you are? You can start over."

"It's my home." Hans's voice broke.

The wargs were emerging from the trees, blue-flame eyes sparking.

He is afraid, Wenzel thought. *He is afraid like all of us. And he'll kill me for it.*

"Hans," Wenzel said, "Greymist Fair isn't your home anymore. The villagers don't *care* if you die. They don't want to kill you because they don't care about you. To them, you're already dead. They stopped thinking about you as soon as you were gone."

Hans's expression began to change. The stiff snarl softened. His eyes widened.

"They're preparing for Yule," Wenzel went on. "It will be a very happy celebration. The happiest in years, since you won't be there. Even Fritz has a new friend. And no one is thinking of you."

The knife lifted from Wenzel's throat. Hans blinked. The tip of his nose was beginning to turn black.

"You had everything," Wenzel said. "You had wealth, good looks, and you were smart. And still they cared more about me than about you. They're waiting for me now. They don't even remember you."

One of the wargs let out a high, keening note, somewhere between hysterical laughter and great sorrow. Hans's head whipped up. He seemed to notice the wargs for the first time. The knife fell into the snow and disappeared.

"But—" he began, and the wargs lunged.

Hans was knocked from Wenzel's chest and enveloped in a savage whirlwind of shadows. Wenzel clawed through the snow to get back to his feet, saw the gift sack against the roots of a tree, and grabbed it. The laces of Heike's boots dug into his neck. Hans shrieked behind him. Wenzel hefted the sack over his shoulder and felt his back sing with pain. The stitches had broken.

Hans's screams were overtaken by the laughter of the wargs.

Wenzel forced his legs to move and began to lope awkwardly through the forest. Heike's boots banged against his chest and his jaw. He didn't know what direction he was going, or how far they'd strayed from the road. All he knew was that he had to keep moving, because the wargs were going to come for him next.

He thought to drop the sack, but didn't. The whole nightmare would be worth nothing if he dropped the gifts. If he didn't at least try.

What made him happy? What made him forget Death?

His inn. It was *his* now, and he took care of it, and he loved having gatherings in the common room and visitors in the rooms. He liked providing for the people there. He liked being someone who the village relied on. He would not give that up for all the faraway adventures in the world.

The wargs caught up to him, flashing from tree to tree.

Heike. She was his first true friend, his best friend, and she had always made the world less scary. When they were together, he felt purely himself, as if she was able to see into the very core of his being. When she laughed, he forgot what was troubling him, if only for a moment. She looked out for him, and he looked out for her, and he loved her. Being with her, even if they went no farther than the fireplace, was an adventure of its own.

The forest burned with blue fire. Its tongues licked at Wenzel's heels.

And his name. His name *now*, not the one that had been yelled at him as a child. His parents had given him options, and he had picked out Wenzel himself. He liked his name. He liked himself. He liked his village. He liked his life. He liked *being alive*. He wanted to stay that way.

Run straight ahead and think of home.

Back screaming in pain, shoulders aching, sweat freezing on his brow, Wenzel thought of Greymist Fair and ran. His legs straightened, his stride grew longer. Trees bent out of his way. Snow burst from his path before his feet hit the ground.

The wargs began to lag behind. They were all around him, then they were only to the sides, then they were behind. Then they were gone, and the trees opened before him. He emerged by the hill on which Heike's cottage sat. There was the inn, the windows lit against the dusk. The village sprawled beyond it, deserted, but also not swarming with wargs.

Heike threw open the inn's back door before he reached it and caught him as he barreled inside. A cushion of other bodies and arms and hands caught them before they could fall to the floor. Someone kicked the door shut. Many voices spoke at once, and Heike was holding his face and asking if he was okay, and all Wenzel could think to do was drop the gift sack and kiss her. Surprised, she kissed him back. The cacophony of questions and arguments was replaced by a stunned cheer and a round of laughter.

"I think I got the new shirt bloody," Wenzel muttered into Heike's hair as the two of them were shuttled into the common area.

"I'll make you another one," she replied quietly, sounding like she might never be upset again.

five

The inn's kitchens were put to work roasting cuts of boar and turkey, warming pies that had miraculously survived the run back to the village. The evergreen in the corner was decorated with bells, cranberries, and wooden carvings of the moon, sun, and stars. The musicians who had brought their instruments from the now-vanished castle began playing near the fire. Stuffed dolls and wooden toys were distributed amongst the children.

There were wargs outside, and Death, but thoughts of them had been banished for the evening. Every candle in the inn was lit, every corner of the common room occupied. Ada Bosch corralled the children to the area around the tree. Gottfried told hunting stories to a gaggle of young men and women, with The Duke stretched out between his legs. Elma Klein and her husband, Norbert, carried mead and wine up from the cellar, and Oswald and Gabi helped distribute it. Dagny and Johanna pulled Godric into the kitchen to help the many cooks reach high shelves, open sealed jars of preserves, and carry the heavy cast-iron kettles. Fritz and Altan could be spied standing unobtrusively in a corner, both looking for some way to help that wouldn't make them more of a burden, keeping each other company.

Wenzel thought that was quite a noble job. No one should be without a friend during Yule. He sat in one of the tall armchairs beside the fire, Heike beside him. His back had been restitched and bandaged, and then Gabi had forced the two of them to relax and not move again for the rest of the night. Wenzel had no problem following that order. He had mead in one hand and Heike's hand in the other, and he was listening to Gottfried's stories with the blissful passivity of the exhausted and tipsy. Heike was already asleep, despite the clamor.

They both woke to eat. Nothing had tasted half so good in his life as what he ate that night, and he had two helpings before sleep took him. He woke again to raucous singing and Fritz and Altan dancing atop one of the tables, their faces red and their movements less than graceful. They had found their way to be helpful; entertainment was as good as anything else.

Wenzel looked over and found Heike smiling at him. He smiled back. She closed her eyes. He did, too.

When he opened them again, it was the early hours of the morning. Some had migrated upstairs to sleep or find quieter rooms; others had passed out right on the common room floor. Many of the children were asleep around the tree with toys still in their hands. Fritz and Altan were picking at a shared plate of food, talking quietly together, red-faced and flirtatious. Gottfried, Ulrich, and Elma were smoking pipes by the fire.

Heike was standing by the window, looking out. With not a small amount of effort, Wenzel levered himself out of the chair and went to stand beside her.

She pointed. "There. Do you see it? Next to the well. Wait for the clouds to pass again."

It took several moments, but eventually moonlight spilled across Greymist Fair. Snow glittered. Next to the well in the center of the village square stood Death, impossibly tall and pale, with wargs heeled at their feet.

"Didn't we do enough? We celebrated Yule. We put everything right," Wenzel said. "No one is scared anymore. They should be gone."

Heike's eyebrows creased. She tapped at her lower lip. "I was thinking, while you were in the forest. Death comes for us all, eventually. Forgetting your fear of it can help for a time, and you can live, but . . . Death is not evil. We will all go with Death one day. We don't have to fear them until then, but we also shouldn't have to ignore them. Death exists, just as we do. This place is Death's home just as it's ours."

"It was Hans's home, too," Wenzel said.

"Yes." Heike sighed and looked at him. "And Hans decided he was more important than his home. There was no living in harmony with Hans. But has anyone given Death that same chance?"

Wenzel twisted a lock of her hair around his finger. "You want to go talk to them?"

"Only if you come with me," she said. "I don't want either of us to go alone anymore."

He took her hand. "Then let's go."

They walked into the night hand in hand. Death watched them approach. The wargs, enough of them to turn the village square black, waited with a quivering kind of energy. Wenzel squeezed Heike's hand and got a squeeze in return. They stopped six feet from Death. Wenzel got a sudden, overwhelming feeling; in his mind he saw the body of a dead bird splayed on the ground, its feathers and flesh rotting away, its bones sinking to dirt. But then wildflowers bloomed in the soil where it had lain, and they grew free and tall. The winter came and the flowers died, and then grass grew anew through the snow. Over and over, death to life to death again, until the changing itself became beautiful.

Heike said, "You must be cold, standing out here."

Death said, "I do not feel the cold. Why have you come? I know you do not fear me now. I never wanted anyone to fear me. But I will have all of you one day."

"We know," said Heike. "And everyone in the village will return to fearing you when Yule is over. If you would like that to change, I think we can help you. Greymist Fair is your home, isn't it?"

Death's dark eyebrows pressed together over black-lake eyes. "Yes."

"And we have never welcomed you, have we?" Heike went on.

"No one does," Death said. "I am the end of all things in this world."

"But you're also the beginning," said Wenzel, surprised by his own voice. Death seemed surprised as well. "Without you there is no change. You make room for the new."

"I do," said Death. Their expression smoothed out as they looked at Wenzel. "So many don't understand."

"They can," Heike said, "if you can be patient with them. All of us have work we do, and it's good work. Necessary work. Sometimes it can be a heavy burden, but being with others makes it lighter." Heike looked to Wenzel. "Maybe we could become friends. But that won't happen while we hate or fear each other."

Death's robes, as dark as the night, seemed to shiver. "Why would you welcome me? I killed my last companion because he lied to me. I have tried to kill your neighbors. I killed your mother and father."

Heike started, blinking through her confusion. Then, taking a deep and shuddering breath, she gathered herself up and said, "You did, and I can't forgive you for that. But even you don't have the power to change the past, and we can't govern you with our laws or our punishments. All that we can do from here is move forward together. You are welcome to visit me whenever you like, as long as you remain civil to my guests and friends and neighbors. We can talk and have tea, like friends do, and when my time comes, you can take me."

"The same for me," Wenzel said. "Come and stay in the inn whenever you like. I'll make you dinner. I love having someone to take care of."

Death's expression wavered with hope and doubt.

"The others will not agree with this," they said. "They will not accept me."

"They will," Heike said, "eventually. But just as we're

extending this trust to you, you must extend it to them. You can't threaten them or harm them. You have to show them that there is nothing to fear."

"If they do not fear me, they will laugh at me," Death said, lip beginning to curl. "They will call me a joke—"

Heike sighed and said patiently, "Maybe, yes. But if you are kind to them, if you help them, if you show that you are trying to be a good neighbor and trying to get to know them, they *will* come around. Wenzel and I will help."

"But there are two things you must do." Wenzel held up two fingers. "One: You must promise you will not hunt those who continue to fear you. Because they will, and you know why they will, and it isn't wrong for them to feel that way. Two: You must release the wargs. They're our friends, our family; they aren't for you to use."

Death looked stricken. "But the wargs are all I have."

"They never killed in the old stories," said Heike. "They're supposed to be guides to lead those who wander. They will still be there for you, but you can't control them the way you have."

Death paused, stiff, then reluctantly turned to the army of wargs in the village square. "I thought for so long that this was the way. But even Luther said I was selfish." They paused for a time, then said quietly, "He was right." Death turned back. Tears rimmed their eyes. "You're sure the villagers will come to accept me?"

There was fear in their voice.

"I'm positive," Heike said. "You'll outlast all of us, and all of our children, and our children's children. I can't promise how long it will take, but there will come a day when we will forget that we ever fought with you. You will be as much a part of this village as the stonework or the fields."

Another moment passed, and then Death's head inclined. The wargs looked up, thousands of pairs of eyes burning, and then, all at once, their nervous quivering stopped. One by one, wargs began to disappear into the darkness until there was only one sitting beside Death, looking up into their pale face. Death looked back at it, crying, and said, "I'm sorry, little one." Then that warg, too, got up and vanished into the darkness.

"I swear," Death said, "not to threaten or harm any person in this village."

Heike held out her free hand. "Now come. It's cold out here."

"I told you, I do not feel the cold."

"I wasn't talking about the weather," said Heike.

"Inside?" Death asked. "During Yule?"

"No better time," Wenzel replied. "There's plenty of food, everyone is exhausted and drunk, and they'll feel better once they know you're not standing outside with the wargs any-more."

Death looked doubtful but took Heike's offered hand. As soon as they did, Death no longer seemed impossibly tall or so very corpse-like. Their circlet of antlers bloomed with linden leaves instead of thorns. The impenetrable chill in the air faded and became the subtle warmth on the cusp of spring, the first scents of a world waking up. To Wenzel, Death and Heike looked like mirrors of one another. Not a dark and a light, but two sides of the same circle, joined again to make a whole.

Wenzel led the way back to the inn, and Heike and Death followed.

HOME
AGAIN

A road leads into a dark forest. It comes from a village some travelers never see. The village is not meant for everyone. To the people who live there, it is safety; it is family; it is home.

Death walks the road beside a girl and boy. The girl is living sunlight; the boy is a flower blooming vividly under her gaze. The village is their home, all of them, and they are returning from a journey. Following them through the forest are a host of souls that have come before them, shepherding them safely to their destination.

The girl stops and looks into the trees. She can sense them there: her mother and father. She never really knew either of them, but she's not sure anyone ever fully knows their parents.

The boy takes her hand and pulls her along. His love overflows him. It always will. He has come through the worst times and seen a better world, and he's dedicated to keeping it.

As they walk, Death hums a tune. It's a popular rhyme with the children of the village, and the boy picks it up, adding a jauntiness that wasn't there before. The girl soon joins in. As they approach the outskirts of the village, Death stops. So do the boy and girl. They hold their hands out. Death hesitates, afraid.

Everyone in Greymist Fair knows Death. They know Death takes the ones they love. Death strips away the color in the world. Death is vengeful and harsh.

"It's all they know," the girl says, gazing at the path Death has walked, where wildflowers sprout from the thawing earth. "We'll teach them something new."

And they do.

Acknowledgments

Thank you, as always, to my agent Louise Fury and her team, including Kristin Smith. Thank you also to the Bent Agency for always being supportive.

Thank you to my editor, Virginia Duncan, and everyone else at Greenwillow and HarperCollins: Sylvie Le Floc'h, Tim Smith and the copyeditors, and Taylan Salvati.

Thank you THANK YOU to Julia Iredale, who designed the stunning cover for the American edition of this book.

Thank you to all my writer friends. I wish I had space to mention each and every one of you.

Thank you to the librarians, teachers, and booksellers who work so hard to get the right books to the right readers, and have been so gracious to invite me to speak in their spaces.

And of course thank you to my family. And to Chad, who watches me drink pickle juice and still likes me. And to Gus and Carl, my good boys.